STEN AND THE MUTINEERS

THE STEN SERIES

STEN AND THE MUTINEERS

ALLAN COLE

Based on the Novel Series by Allan Cole and Chris Bunch.

WILDSIDE PRESS

For Kathryn, my love, my everything
and
Drew And Vicky
whose love and care saw me through
and
Scott Braun
who gave me the strength to carry on.

Published by Wildside Press LLC.
www.wildsidepress.com

AUTHOR'S NOTE

This tale is set between Sten #2, *The Wolf Worlds*, and Sten #3, *The Court of a Thousand Suns*, when Sten was still a young Mantis officer.

CHAPTER ONE

THE COVENANTER

Mahoney started up the cargo ramp, then stepped aside as two Psaurs loomed out of the swirling nighttime fog, back claws clicking against the ramp, sawtooth-rimmed jaws unhinged in what Mahoney thought might be anger. But who could tell with the Psaurs? To most beings, their natural look was homicidal.

When they reached Mahoney, they paused, two pairs of fierce red eyes peering down at him.

The tallest one hiccupped, then slurred, "Lookin' for th' *Covenanter*, cheena?"

The shorter one gave what Mahoney could have sworn was a girlish giggle—as issued through a rusty exhaust pipe—then said, "'Course he is, Ursie, baby. Can'tcha see that look he's got? Wants nothing better'n get drunk and take a Joygirl for a grav ride."

She looked closer at Mahoney. "Or, mebbe a…joyboy?"

Reflexively, Mahoney shook his head. The lady Psaurs shrugged. "Makes no diff' to us, cheena."

Mercifully, her companion broke in. Pointed. "Straight up the ramp. Escalator on left. Won't see it. Too dark. But you can hear it. Bad bearings. Sounds like a stepped on Ceres cat. Head for th' cat. Then stairs. Careful with stairs."

He made a zip/splat motion with one broad claw… "Greasy. Slip and fall. Red sign. Mebbe not see in fog. Hail th' house. Somebody'll come and getcha."

Mahoney thanked them and started up the ramp. Behind him, the lady Psaurs called out, "Tell Janiz that Ursie 'n his mate sentcha. Our Janiz'll set you right."

Without those directions, Mahoney would have been lost in the warren that was Port Soward, the busiest spaceport on Prime World—which meant the entire Empire.

On top of that, the Covenanter was at the arse end of the arse end of Soward. Mahoney had to negotiate a three-level architectural mess of warehouses, tool shops, and repair bays all cloaked in a dense nighttime fog.

Once he thought he spotted a red light glittering through the fog and pushed on. But he kept losing sight of the glitter and found himself moving in a circle.

Finally, in total frustration and feeling like a potato-gobbling Irish fool, he raised his head and bellowed:

"Ahoy the house!"

A moment later he sensed a presence and instinctively reached out to see what it was. But before his fingers could touch, a door opened. Glaring light and loud sound poured over him. A blur and then out of the glare stepped a remarkably beautiful women.

He was momentarily rendered speechless by her presence. Finally, he blurted, "You must be Janiz."

Her smile added to her stunning beauty. "That's me," she said. "Janiz Kerleh. Chief bartender, cook and bottle washer."

She opened the door wider, stepping aside and motioning for him to enter.

"This way, Sr. Mahoney," she said. "Engineer Raschid is expecting you."

* * * *

Hard to find though it might be, The Covenanter was packed arses to carapace with beings from every corner of the Empire. Be they ET or human, all seemed to be having a boisterously boozy good time. Mahoney even saw traditional enemies like the Suzdal and Jochians competing in round-buying generosity. The main thing seemed to be that they were all space rats together, from greasy engine devils and brawny boson's mates to tight-fisted merchant captains and rumpled techs, who all seemed to be wearing corrective lenses, whether they had faces or not.

The bar was decorated Antique Space Age style, with mysterious bits of machinery, oddly shaped tools, and colorful emblems and banners from the distant past where—as the old timers liked to say—beings were beings and interstellar jumps frequently ended in maiming or even death.

As Mahoney followed Janiz, the crowd magically parted before her. And what a magical sight she made: all that bounty contained in a short emerald green tunic, cut low to better display her creamy white charms. Long legs sheathed in thigh-high boots. Fiery red hair spilling over pale shoulders.

On one side of the Covenanter stood a long bar—made of a rock-hard material so black it seemed to devour light rather than reflect it. In the center was a jumble of tables and chairs of both human and ET design. Booths lined the other three walls. One of the booths, Mahoney noted, had a drawn curtain. As they approached, he spotted a brass place plate at the base, which read: *Booth C. Reserved.*

Janiz called out, "Raschid, honey. Your guest is here."

The curtain parted. Lounging in the booth was The Eternal Emperor.

"Slide on in, Ian," the Emperor said. "The narcobeer's fine."

The Emperor's spymaster grinned. "Music to an Irishman's heart, boss," he said and slid on in.

CHAPTER TWO

THE ETERNAL EMPEROR

As chief of the Emperor's Mercury Corps—along with its super secret blackarts ancillary, Mantis Section—General Ian Mahoney was one of the few people who knew that his boss was wont to—as he put it—"go walkabout" without any notice.

He'd disguise himself as an ordinary citizen to embark on these mini-journeys. He favored the guise of a chief engineer, hinting that such a role came from his very distant past.

How distant? No one really knew. All histories that dealt with the subject strictly avoided that sort of speculation—much less scholarly study.

There were rumors—the sort of rumors only a spymaster would hear—that certain historians who expressed interest in that area had been contacted by a rich benefactor and steered into other fascinating subjects of study with guarantees of fully-funded research. The few who resisted in the spirit of academic freedom tended to disappear and never be heard from again.

The walkabout business was the Emperor's way of what he called "rejoining the herd."

"What everybody's really talking about is what I want to know," he'd say during one of his frequent booze sessions with Mahoney.

"Are they working? Kids doing okay? I know they think the government's full of drakh—and it sure as clot is—but are they really mad about it? Or just blowing steam? I want to see it up close and personal, not through the filter of one of Parliament's functionaries."

And so the supreme ruler Mahoney was presently looking at wore a merchantman's uniform that had survived many orbits, with tattered Chief Engineer tabs on either shoulder and a greasy

Space Workers Union seniority badge pinned to his chest. He did not resemble anyone the royal courtiers of Prime World had ever seen.

The Eternal Emperor was a big man. Handsome. Strong features, marked by steely blue eyes that had a slight Asian cast to them. Age? A drinking buddy might guess thirty-five going on forty.

When the Emperor spoke, he sometimes used unfamiliar words—words that when Mahoney looked them up would turn out to be from an age so distant it was all but lost to memory.

Sometimes when asked a question he'd drift off into extended thought, as if the question had triggered some memory so buried in the past that he'd have to peel back the layers century by century.

His moods could be mercurial, although he was always deadly calm in a crisis. At the moment, the Emperor looked cheery—a man looking forward to a boozy night on the town. Ending with some nice soft and fragrant company.

Janiz spoke up, startling Mahoney, who'd momentarily forgotten she was there.

She said, "You look like you could use another, Rashid, honey." She turned to Ian. "How about you, sweetie? What's your preference?"

Mahoney nodded at the Emperor's setup. "Same as the boss," he said. "Narcobeer with a synthalk back."

Janiz laughed. Ian liked the sound of it. She said, "You a barrel bombardier too, honey?"

Mahoney frowned. "Barrel bombardier?"

"That's what he calls them," she said, nodding at the Emperor. "Barrel bombs. Drops the shot glass into the mug of beer—bombs away! So I named him the Barrel Bombardier."

They all laughed, and then Janiz collected the Emperor's empty glasses and ankled toward the bar. Mahoney couldn't help but gaze lustfully at those swaying hips.

"She's all that…and more, Ian," the Eternal Emperor said, as if reading his thoughts.

Mahoney swung back, feeling a bit guilty. He said, "Is she… uh…I mean, are you and she…you know…"

"On and off," the Emperor said. "More off than on these days. We had quite the fling twenty years or so ago. Met her on walkabout. She was taking business classes, or some such, by day. Little Joygirl work at night. Down on her luck when we met. Run over by a bad choice in boyfriends, or something. I was down myself. It was a bad time in the throneroom, I'll tell you that.

"Anyway, we clicked. Got her a place. Some off-the-books government work. And told her I'd mostly be off on merchant runs and I'd see her when I could. Meanwhile, she could do what she liked.

"Eventually passions cooled, as they say, but we remained friends. So I set her up in business." He waved around the room. "We own it together, with me playing the part of the very silent partner."

Janiz was coming back through the crowd, carrying a tray of drinks.

Mahoney said, "So you and she…are…uh…"

The Emperor laughed. "Sorry, Ian. Out of luck tonight." He grew serious. "They're getting to me, Ian."

Mahoney didn't have to ask who *they* were. "Yeah, I know, boss."

"And Janiz… Well, she has a way of…"

He let the rest trail off as Janiz reached them and started unloading her tray. She looked at Mahoney. "You look lonely, honey," she said. "Some silly woman disappoint you?"

Mahoney sighed. "If wishes were wings, as my granny used to say." And he thought—dear old granny was Irish and knew how hopeless that would be.

But then, the whole situation suddenly struck Mahoney as incredibly funny. He started laughing and kept on laughing until it turned to coughing and the Emperor was slapping him on the back.

"Drink up, Ian," he said. "A barrel bomb will cure what ails you."

And so he dropped the shotglass of synthalk into the mug of narcobeer, then chugging it down in one long pull.

He set the empty mug down. Burped. "I've taken my medication," he said, "and I feel much better now."

More laughter. Finally, Janiz ankled away to tend her other customers.

Silence.

Then the Emperor reached under the table and palmed a button. The curtain closed and all sound from the outside vanished. Mahoney realized this was state of the state of the art security stuff. Impervious to electronic penetration.

The Eternal Emperor leaned across the table. "Now, tell me, Ian," he said. "What the clot are we going to do about those damned mutineers?"

CHAPTER THREE

THE MISSION

"I know the situation is an embarrassment, Your Highness," Mahoney said, dropping all informality the moment the curtains shut off the outside world. "But we can't just send in an Imperial Cruiser and snatch them up."

"I don't mind a little embarrassment, General," the Emperor said, "as long as I have a willing scapegoat I can blame it on. Some functionary who will fall on his sword for the greater good of the Empire and a guaranteed lifetime of wealth."

"Yes sir," was all Mahoney said. When the boss wanted the floor, it was best to give it to him.

"For someone to steal an entire space-train of Imperium X would be blow enough," the Emperor said. "But we'd just be talking piracy, and the guys with the big com units are all insured for pirates. It would shake the drakh out of the insurance companies, but I could shore them up with a little creative bookkeeping.

"Meanwhile, I'd send a cruiser—hell, I might send a whole clotting fleet—and I'd kick some pirate ass and get the Imperium X back. Put it in the royal treasury to offset all those credits I'd spent."

He sighed, took a pull on the mug, then said, "But it wasn't pirates that stole a 125-kilometer-long ore train. No, it was a group of my very own citizens. True blue and loyal Imperial merchantmen who proved to be vipers. Traitors." And he almost spat the last—"Mutineers."

Once again, silence reigned.

Then the Emperor sighed. "I'm done ranting, Ian," he said. "Now, tell me what we're up against. What are their latest demands?"

Mahoney said, "Sir, they claim they've got a handsome offer

from those rogues over in the Possnet Sector. A fortune in credits, Your Majesty, plus protection from us."

"I'm not surprised," the Emperor said. "All that Imperium X. The second most valuable commodity in my Empire."

Mahoney nodded. It went without saying that the *most* valuable commodity was AM2. The stuff that fueled the Empire. But without Imperium X as the shield, Anti-Matter Two was useless. And without AM2—the ultimate energy source—the Empire would collapse.

He said, "What they want is for us to better the deal." After a pause, he added, "And they want amnesty."

The Emperor glared at Mahoney. "Amnesty?" he said. "I'll give them amnesty. I'll have them skinned alive. I'll have them drawn and quartered. I'll have them—" He broke off. Drained his glass. Muttered to himself.

Mahoney frowned. "Drawn and quartered, sir?"

The Emperor waved the question away. "I hope you have a plan, Ian." His tone was icy.

"I do, sir," Mahoney said. "At least the beginnings of one. As you know, sir, if they spot us coming, they'll just go over to the pirates. Sell their goods and pickle their livers for the rest of their lives."

"Which is why I'm meeting with you right now, Ian," the Emperor said, "and not a table-full of generals and admirals. We need sneaky, here, and you give good sneaky."

"Well, sir," Ian said, "if you really want sneaky, it so happens we have a Mantis team in the area. Just over by the Lupus Cluster."

The Emperor frowned, then remembered. "That young lieutenant," he said. "The one who handled the Wolf Worlds matter so well. His name was…Sten. Yes. That's it. Sten."

"The very man, sir," Mahoney said.

The Emperor frowned. "I thought I had him promoted to captain," he said.

"You did, sir."

"And wasn't I going to put him in charge of my Gurkha guard?"

"You were, sir."

The Emperor's brow cleared. "Ah, I recall now. All that trouble broke out in the Frontier Worlds. Greedy mining companies. Smugglers. Pirates. So I thought it best to freeze him in place.

Keep him handy for when we needed him."

"Yessir. That was the decision, sir."

"How wise of me," the Emperor said.

"Indeed, sir," Mahoney said. He paused, then added. "I thought it best not to mention his impending promotion until the situation changed, sir. Besides, the seasoning will do him good."

"If I were young Sten," the Emperor said, "I'd be pretty ticked off that I didn't get any recognition for cleaning up that Lupus Cluster mess."

Mahoney sighed. "He probably is, sir," he said. "But he's a soldier and has to learn to just suck it up. Besides, I'll make it up to him later."

The Emperor shrugged. "Well, ticked off or not, he's just where we need him, and he's the perfect choice to clean up this mess."

"Yessir," Mahoney said.

"Okay, Ian, with Sten we have a good start." The Emperor said. "Talk to him and see what that nasty Mantis brain of his can come up with. Give him *carte blanche* to act as he sees fit."

"Yes sir," Mahoney said. "Right away, sir."

He started to rise. The Emperor motioned for him to sit. He sat.

"One more things," the Emperor said.

"Yes, your Highness?"

"That ship's captain? The one the mutineers took hostage?"

Mahoney remembered. Grimaced. "Gregor, sir," he said. "Captain Gregor."

When he'd checked the files, he'd found that Gregor was one of the most incompetent morale killers in the Royal Navy. The only reason he'd had this job was because of the Imperium X boom in the Fringe Regions.

The Imperial Navy was so overstretched that even the dregs were swept up into positions of authority. And Gregor perfectly fit the definitions of dregs. With him as captain, no wonder the crew mutinied.

"Right, Gregor," the Emperor said. "It seems he's got a rich daddy who wants him back."

After reading the file, Mahoney couldn't understand why. Gregor was such a scrote it was hard to imagine him being the apple of any father's eye. However, this rich daddy was one Lord Wichman, who built and owned exclusive resorts, casinos, and sporting facilities all over the Empire, along with countless other enterprises, ranging from a line of faux gourmet food items such as soya steak (an oxymoron if Mahoney ever heard one), to some very bad wine and liqueurs that had superb ratings from influential critics on the take.

Naturally, Wichman's had a huge ego and plastered his name on enormous signs and banners on all his holdings.

Mahoney sighed. Sometimes sentient beings were beyond comprehension. However, Ian knew the Emperor had an even lower opinion of the man than he did. And if his boss deemed it necessity to free Gregor from the clutches of the mutineers, he obviously had very good reasons for it.

"And the amnesty, sir?" he asked. "Do we agree to that?"

The Emperor waved that away. "Sure, sure," he said. "Tell young Sten he can definitely offer amnesty."

CHAPTER FOUR

THE BEAUTY AND THE SCOTSMAN

A gritty wind scratched Sten's faceplate as he peered up at the sign.

REC AREA 477

"Ah think some bampot musta' made a wee mistake here, laddie," Alex said.

Sten sighed. Unfortunately, the idiot in question was standing next to him.

"No mistake," he said. "This is the place."

Behind them, he heard the scrape of a gravcab lifting off. Sten turned, clumsy in his Hostile Atmosphere Suit, hoping against clotting hope he could hail it back. If he failed, it would be at least a day before they could get transport out of this wretched place.

Unfortunately, as he signaled, the gravcab was already over the blood red mountain peaks on to its next hire.

Sten shivered despite his heated HA suit. Or, maybe because of it. The wretched thing had been the only one left on the rack in his size. Imperial PX's weren't well supplied in this outback.

A cold wind flowed down from the peaks across an ancient seabed as red as the mountains. Deep carbon-black canyons cut across the land, with huge ebony boulders stacked crazily, one upon the other—left there when the seas boiled away long ago. The fact that MP914 was a working mining planet was underscored with some regularity. The land was pocked with enormous vents, charred like the bores of ancient gunpowder cannons. The purpose of those vents soon became apparent when the ground began to shake under them, and then a huge column of fire and smoke burst from the very bowels of the planet, boiling against azure skies.

Around them, the wind picked up glittering red sand and flung it against the rocks in booming scarlet waves.

"Hokay, hokay, laddie," Alex said. "Ah don't blame ya' if yer thinkin'—'away an boil yer heed, Alex Kilgour.' But mebbe, jist mebbe, it's nae as bad as it 'pears."

Sten turned back to consider: The scene before them looked nothing like what they had been led to expect.

The other bumpot in this equation was the Leave Clerk. Corporal McKenna—she of the flowing blond hair, the curvaceous body, the flashing eyes—had beguiled Alex as she painted an exotic word-picture of the wonders that awaited them at Rec Area 477.

Sten had never seen Kilgour so enamored. Doting on every word that spilled from McKenna's lovely Scottish lips. Corporal McKenna played them a vid of a sparkling white Grecian palace, spread over several kilometers, floating gloriously on the "wine-dark" sands of Mining Planet 914.

She explained that the benevolent mining companies—whose motto was "Morale Comes First"—spared no expense when it came to entertaining the miners, contractors, and many other trades and professions it took to keep the Imperium X flowing to the Eternal Emperor's vast storage centers.

The rec area on MP914 was only one of many such entertainment centers throughout this economically vital mining region.

But Corporal McKenna, who could pour it on like a Gaelic poet, insisted Rec Area 477, was the most wonderful of all. Offering the strongest drinks, the most delicious food, as well as the most glamorous and eager joygirls and joyboys.

"Best of all," she had said, "its spirited gambling—with the best odds—is beyond compare."

The beautiful McKenna had been so eloquent, so enthusiastic, that the thought niggled at the back of Sten's brain that maybe the corporal had a commissioning deal with the entertainment center.

Alex would have none of it. "Oh, my puir, puir laddie," he'd said in a brief moment when they were left alone to confer. "Ah'm ashamed ay ye. Sech a suspicious mind. Hoo can ye doubt sech a brammer lass, with only our best interests at heart?"

"Think you're going to score with her, don't you?" Sten teased.

"Weel, Ah would nae rule it out, laddie," he'd answered. "Me mum al'ays said Ah was a braw figure ay a cheil."

Alex was a heavy worlder—as wide as he was tall and all of it dense muscle. But as for presenting a "braw figure"—well, only a loving mother could have described his less than Grecian form as such.

However, Alex was Sten's best friend. A friend who had saved his life countless times, and so who was Sten to spoil his friend's chances with the lovely Corporal McKenna?

But as he examined the place where they were supposed to spend the next e-week, he realized just how apt the saying was that, "no good deed ever goes unpunished."

There was no palace. Natch. Instead, Sten and Alex were standing before the ruins of what Sten thought had once been an in-system passenger ship, with a bulbous nose and stubby winglets.

No doubt some bright mining company Veep had wrangled a bonus for pimping the money-saving idea: instead of scrapping the worn out wreck, they could plunk it down on one of the Fringe Region's mining planets. In this case, MP914.

A little repurposing here and there, and they'd soon have a wondrous gambling hall for their workers. And they could churn their employees' wages back into the company coffers many times over.

As the cold sandy wind rattled and scratched against his HA suit, Sten thought that if Hell was cold instead of hot, it must look a lot like good old MP914.

After the ground tremors subsided, Alex said, "Dae ye suppose a body coods gie a wee narcobeer around here, laddie?"

"If we can't at least get that," Sten said, "I'm going to personally strangle your girlfriend at the Leave Office."

"She's nae me bird," Alex protested.

Sten couldn't help but laugh. "Oh, so she stood you up after all, huh?" he said. "You never let on."

Alex sniffed. "A gentleman ne'er tells," he said.

"Especially when there is nothing to tell," Sten said.

Alex snorted. "Ah'm thirsty," he said, and he took Sten's arm in a steely grip and powered him up the ramp to the forbidding entrance of Rec Area 477.

CHAPTER FIVE

HELL ON WARP DRIVE

Sten and Alex paused long enough for a credit scan to establish their limits, got a medium grade score, and then were escorted into the airlock foyer. There they doffed their HA suits, submitted to a fairly heavy duty weapons scan, and were finally cleared.

Sten had to smile to himself, thinking of the deadly little blade hidden in a fleshy sheath in his arm. Sten had built it from a rare crystal grown in the poisonous atmosphere his fellow Vulcan slaves called Hellworld. Harder and more durable than just about any other known substance, it had a blade one molecule thick.

With a motion of his arm and a flick of his wrist he could cut a throat or slice through a beam of forged steel as easily as the proverbial hot knife cleaves through newly congealed milk fat.

Once they were cleared, another airlock opened to reveal thick double doors. They pushed through, only to be hit with a veritable tsunami of sound—a thunderous cacophony of screaming, shouting beings scrambling desperately to jam in as much clotting fun as possible in a very short time. When their leave was over, it would be back to another contracted E-year in the Imperium X mines of MP914.

Gambling bots pimped the odds in so many languages it was as if someone had tipped over the legendary Tower of Babel and all the words had spilled out. Pleasure-room shills piped up here and there, boasting of their fleshy wares.

Yes, cheenas, there was truly something for every being's pleasure on offer here. No matter if you were endowed with two legs, eight legs, tentacles, or claws. No matter what sexuality, or combination of sexualities you were born with. No matter how sexually sophisticated you were, there was not one act or position illustrated in the *Kumasutra for All Beings* that could not be performed here.

Satisfaction guaranteed.

Meanwhile, promo machines added to the adrenaline-charged atmosphere, hooting and hollering and grinding their gears, while trumpeting the news of the latest BIG WINNERS.

Beings from all over the Empire packed the gigantic hall, milling about in mass confusion and supercharged excitement. If it weren't for the brawny security bots that roamed the floor, chaos would have soon shown its ugly face.

Sten was so overwhelmed by it all that he staggered.

"Steady, young Sten," Alex said. And he felt Kilgour's big hand on his elbow. With his other hand he snatched a drink off a barbot tray and delivered it to Sten, who gingerly tested it.

"Stregg, by God," he croaked.

He chugged it down and felt the fiery liquid burn away the confusion.

Stregg was the belly-and-brain burning drink that the Bhor chieftain, Otho, had introduced him to when his minions joined forces with Sten's Mantis team to topple the religious zealots ruling the Wolf Worlds.

Alex fetched him another, and he inhaled that as well. By a Bhor father's frozen buttocks, it was good. And by a Bhor mother's icy beard, the world about him began to make some sense. Just as it made sense that he had been so disoriented in the first place. After all, he and Alex—along with Ida and Doc—had been TDY'd to convoy escort duty for many months now, with no other company, and no apparent end to their Fringe Region tour within official, or unofficial, sight.

Sometimes they felt that perhaps the great victory they had won in the Lupus Cluster had been pyrrhic to the extreme. And instead of honors and awards they'd been condemned to endless patrols and boring scouting missions for the Imperium X space-trains.

As time dripped endlessly by, Sten had even began to feel betrayed by Mahoney, his supposed mentor, who'd rescued him from a short and miserable life as a slave laborer on Vulcan—the factory world of his birth.

But had he really been rescued? Or had Mahoney merely used him to foil Baron Thoresen's conspiracy against the Eternal Emperor, before feeding Sten into the Imperial military's always hungry maw?

True, Mahoney had engineered Sten's career as a member of the super elite Mantis Section, turning him into a skilled saboteur, assassin, and general all around disrupter of the Order of Things.

So what had happened?

Why were his skills and the skills of his shipmates and fellow Mantis operatives being squandered in such a manner?

Amid all this lonely tedium, the self doubt grew. And he was starting to feel downright mutinous when suddenly their ship, the *Storm*, had staged a bit of mechanical and technical mutiny of its own.

The little Bulkeley class attack boat was overdue on every maintenance schedule deemed necessary by her manufacturers and Sten and the others had done all they could to keep her running and operational.

Then things got so bad that their superiors had grudgingly approved minimal repair and refurbishment work. Their tight-fisted bosses had consoled their bureaucratic selves by ordering the team to bleed off some of their overdue leave.

The idea of vacationing in a region many light years from any civilized fun was ludicrous. But orders were orders and there was nothing to be done about it except whine and complain, the right of soldiers everywhere and everywhen.

Ida and Doc had elected to stay with the *Storm*.

Ida holed up with a like-minded geek she met at a spaceport bar and the two were off gaming the Imperial commodities markets.

Doc's idea of a forced good time was to blow his budget on a supply of vintage plasma, then repair to his cabin for a good and bloody drunk, while composing epic Blyrchynaus poetry.

Alex had different ideas. In no uncertain terms, he let it be known just how tired he was of cramming his heavy-worlder's body into the miniscule living space allotted aboard the *Storm*.

Sergeant Alex Kilgour, late of the planet New Edinburgh, wanted out, by God! He yearned to mingle with other beings. Eat something other than Dry Pack Meals. Quaff a brew or three. Dance with some bonny lassies.

In short, he said, "Ah want to party!"

The problem, Sten had argued, was the only places in reach were on the rough and tumble mining worlds, where fortunes were being made and lost grubbing for Imperium X on some of the most inhospitable worlds in the empire.

"Probably end up on the floor every night," Sten grumbled, "from drink and fisticuffs."

In the end, Sten had relented and they'd been conned by a pretty blonde with flashing eyes and a short tartan kilt to choose Rec Area 477 as their playground.

And now, as he looked about at the mad scene, he was sorry as sorry could be.

But just as he was about to turn to his friend and beg that they call the whole clotting thing off, another barbot tray rolled past and he reflexively scooped up a mug while Kilgour liberated another.

"What the clot," Sten said. "I've gotten drunk in worse drakh holes than this."

Kilgour roared laughter, crashed his mug against Sten's, and they both drained their glasses and started moving through the crowd.

A couple of barbot trays later they began making woozy sense of their surroundings, pausing here and there to take a chance at a Chuckaluck bot, or a roll of the holo-dice.

A largish Ceph was the boss dealer at one table that featured an ancient retro game of Blackjim. The table was shaped like a quarter moon and the Ceph held forth in the slot—four pairs of tentacles dealing rectangular pieces of plas decorated with numbers and pictures.

Two big eyes, perched above a long sharp beak, kept careful watch on the players while she dealt the cards and kept up a patter.

"There's a royal for ya, cheena. Chance another? No? Where's yer scrote, cheena? Where's yer scrote?"

A few more trays later and they were starting to really admire the long-legged Joygirls ankling through the crowd.

"This is all right," he shouted at Alex, as he snagged another drink.

Kilgour cupped a hand to his ear. "What?"

Sten shouted louder. "This is all right!"

Alex shook his head and shouted back: "Ah cannae hear a wuid yer sayin', me wee mucker. Yoo'll hae tae spick looder."

Sten laughed, shook his head helplessly, and motioned for Alex to continue deeper into gaming hall. But then a chilling snarl brought him up short. Immediately followed by a hate-charged odor that made his hair stand on end.

Both the snarl and the odor were frighteningly familiar.

He stepped back, pulling Alex with him, as an ugly little man carrying a large wire cage pushed past them. Sten saw a flash of green scales, a gleam of fangs and claws, and then the man was carrying the cage into a tented room.

Alex leaned close to ask: "What's 'at all aboo, laddie? An' what manner ay beest is 'at? Looks a bit loch a wee T-Rex."

Before Sten could reply, someone in the crowd shouted, "Xypaca fight! Xypaca fight!" Immediately the cry was taken up— "Xypaca, Xypaca, Xypaca"—and a section of the crowd broke off and surged toward tent.

Sten and Alex were momentarily caught up in the craziness, but Kilgour put his heavy-worlder shoulder to it and they broke free. They found themselves in a corner partially shielded from the craziness by a large narcobeer fountain.

"What the clot is a Xypaca?" Alex asked. "An' what are they fightin' abit?"

"They're horrible little scrotes," Sten said. "Twenty centimeters high, or so. But they'll take on anything up to a hundred times their own size. Hate everything, especially each other. When they meet—unless it's the mating season—they'll immediately try to kill each other."

Alex snorted. "Soonds loch a pack ay bludy Campbells."

"Yeah, but they make perfect pit-fighters," Sten said. "The blood-lust crowds love them. And they bet like crazy. Hell, my father spent all our savings on one of those horrible things. Bet his future and ours on it."

"What happened?" Alex asked.

Sten grabbed a mostly clean mug and scooped up narcobeer from the fountain. Drank half of it.

"He won, just like he thought," Sten said. "But ended up losing because he beat the wrong man."

He was drawing in a deep breath, trying to restore his good mood, when a strange group of beings caught his eye.

It was an obvious security detail—guarding some VIP, Sten supposed. There were seven of them. Six formed a wedge, with the seventh in the center. They were coming around the Blackjim tables and were headed toward the Xypaca tent.

He couldn't make out the VIP, but the six were large, heavily muscled beings. Humanoid. Female. Albino-white, with silver hair. They were nearly naked, with black armor modesty swatches guarding the most vulnerable parts.

Sten liked how they handled themselves. Liked how they constantly scanned the crowd for danger. Very professional.

The probing gaze of one of them fell upon Sten. Measured him with glowing pink eyes. No apparent danger. The eyes moved on.

"They're Himmenops," Alex said. "Saw their likes once when ah was a wee lad."

Sten nodded, recalling the odd (to him) beings from one of his Mantis socio-species courses.

Warlike. Restless. Lived in fortressed colonies. An Appian-like all female hive society. All powerful queen. Guarded by a special enhanced breed of Himmenops, called the Zabanya.

"Ah'm surprised tae see them," Kilgour said. "They're usually such loners."

And adventurers too, Sten thought. The minute the Himmenops became technically advanced enough, they'd scattered across the empire. Staking out most the inhospitable but defendable systems, where they took up residence and made their living through interstellar trade, sharp practices, and plain old fashioned piracy.

As if reading his mind, Alex said, "Mus' be some ay th' local Possnet pirates."

"If we weren't on I&I," Sten said, referring to what was popularly known among their fellow troopies as Intercourse & Intoxication, "I'd feel it was our duty to investigate. That's what Mahoney would want."

"An' th' wee General could take a flyin' humph," Alex said. "We're on vacation. As FIGMO as FIGMO can be."

Sten was about to ask Alex what the clot "FIGMO" was when he finally got a clear look at the being the six were guarding.

She was the most stunningly beautiful woman Sten had ever seen.

And she was entirely human.

She was tall, slender, her skin a gleaming ebony, her hair, long sable tresses that spilled over one bare shoulder, her breasts round and firm and high, her hips and thighs a beckoning paradise.

Then in a moment she was gone, disappearing into the tent with her coterie.

Sten stood there a moment. Frozen. Mouth dry. Heart racing. Then he started toward the tent.

"Where ye be goin, laddie?" Alex asked, following him.

"To investigate," Sten shot back.

CHAPTER SIX

THE SCARLET XYPACA

The supercharged blood-sport atmosphere nearly bowled Sten over when he and Alex entered the tent. The air reeked of anger and fear and adrenaline, with that underlying musk of sexual excitement.

In the center of the tent a boisterous crowd was gathered around a regulation Xypaca fighting cage, shouting and cheering as the two occupants went at it fang and claw.

From helping his dad back on Vulcan, Sten knew the exact measurements of the cage: 8.6 meters long, 6.4 meters wide and 3.2 meters height. For a creature only twenty centimeters high, this had seemed excessive to Sten.

His father explained: "Little bustards not only move like lightning, but they can side jump ten meters, no sweat. As far as how high—well, I've seen them hop four meters easy as pork fat through a gray Anser."

"Gray Anser?" Sten had asked, puzzled.

"A goose boy, a goose."

He hadn't bothered asking what pork fat was. Sounded disgusting.

His father had gone on to explain that the wire cage was made of super-hardened plas. "Anything else," his father had said, "and they'll bite right through the cage and maybe take some poor scrote's face off."

Sten could almost hear his mother protest: "Amos! Language!"

His father had laughed and given her a kiss. "The boy's heard worse," he'd said. "Plus he's got a pair himself."

Sten smiled wistfully at the memory of the parental dispute. His mother, father, brother and sister—long dead now, victims of Baron Thoresen's conspiracy.

The crowd's roar brought him back. In the cage, the two Xypacas were locked together, teeth razoring, claws ripping. Blood spatter everywhere. Drawing the crowd closer, despite the shower of blood.

Then came the final moment when one Xypaca saw its chance and, in a barely perceptible strike, tore out its enemy's throat.

Alex was clearly not a newly won over fan of the Xypaca game. He tugged at Sten's sleeve, saying, "Let's get the clot out a here, laddie. This is nae mah idea ay entertainment. Let's find a couple ay bonny lassies, me mucker.

"Make love, nae war, that's th' Kilgour family motto."

Sten shook his head. "In a minute," he said, his mouth going suddenly dry when he spotted his quarry.

The fabulously beautiful woman and her Zabanya guards were in a corner near the Xypaca cages.

Then the ugly little man he'd noticed earlier joined them—carrying a covered cage. A discussion ensued. The woman listened, then waved an imperious hand—her lips forming the words "Show me."

The little man whipped off the cover. And out of the cage came a shriek so blood-curdling that it silenced the crowd.

Everyone turned to see a ball of scarlet fury ripping at the cage with a primeval ferocity that made the woman's burly guards instinctively step back.

But the woman seemed fascinated, rather than frightened—leaning in for a closer look.

It was significantly larger than the other Xypacas and red instead of green. Obviously, the little man was a Xypaca breeder and Sten was witnessing a sale.

His guess was confirmed when he saw the woman motion for one of her guards to pay the man. It must have been a handsome sum, because he practically skipped away.

Then she caught the attention of one of the green vested officials, who hurried over to confer. It was the Oddsmaster. A fight was being arranged.

Sten spotted the probable contender in a nearby cage.

It was nearly as big as the scarlet beast raging in its cage. By now it had been infected by the scent of the red newcomer and was tearing at the bars, trying to get at it.

In a moment, the owner hurried over, followed by the Fightmaster—a meter-and-a-half high Brachy, complete with claws and multiple eyestalks.

The Fightmaster quietly conferred with her colleague, the Oddsmaster, then turned back to the woman and the owner of the green Xypaca.

The haggling commenced, accompanied by much arm and claw waving. The woman clearly wanted a feature match, with no limit stakes. The owner was wary. Sure his Xypaca was good. On most days, the best. But that red Xypaca clearly had him worried.

Finally, odds were settled. Credits banked. The fight scheduled for the feature slot.

Satisfied, the woman turned to watch the death match in progress and was immediately caught up in the action.

Sten thought she evinced the signs of what his dad called a Xypaca junky. He smiled to himself. But in her case, it was in the nicest sense of the word.

A germ of an idea surfaced: how he could meet the woman and get a little intelligence for Mahoney.

"Alex," he said, "what we need now is a nice juicy soy steak. Thin sliced."

"What're you up to, laddie?" Alex asked.

"I'm gonna fix a fight," Sten said. "What else?"

CHAPTER SEVEN

THE PIRATE QUEEN

By the time Alex returned, dripping soy steak juice from the wad of napkins he'd wrapped the bits in, Sten had big-eared enough conversations to gather a little intel about the woman.

Her name was Venatora and she was the boss lady of the most formidable colony of pirates in the Possnet Sector.

The fact that the Himmenops had a human queen, rather than one of their own, only added to her mystery. She was also a keen gambler and would bet on just about anything, up to and including wagering on which head would hit the floor first in a double execution.

It didn't seem to matter that she was wanted everywhere for her crimes—which were legion. Venatora had bribed or intimidated every cop in the region and was obsessively protected by her fanatic followers.

Alex thrust the sopping package at Sten. "Here, ye be, my old mucker," he said. "Tak' th' mingin mess."

Chuckling, Sten refused the package. "Got a job for you sergeant," he said. "A job that will require all your stealthy Mantis skills."

Alex frowned. "What manner a loony business is goin' on in thae wee noggin?" he asked.

"I want you to slip over to the cages," Sten replied, "and while everyone is busy watching the fights, feed the soy strips to the red Xypaca. I want it fat and happy by time the fight is called."

Alex was aghast. "Guid clottin' day, hae ye seenth' size ay those burds?" he said, indicating Venatora's guardswomen. "They'll rip mah heed aff an' drakh in mah neck."

"That was my thinking as well," Sten said. "As a trained and certified professional, my advice to you is…don't get caught."

Grumbling, Alex headed for the cages. Meanwhile, Sten slipped out of the tent to reclaim the semi-quiet spot near the narc-obeer fountain.

He got on the horn with Ida.

"Sten, you clottin' clot," she grumbled, "why are you bothering me? I'm on vacation, remember? Drakh, we're all on vacation! Go get laid or something. Leave me the clot alone."

"You making money?" Sten asked.

Ida snorted. "What a stupid question. Of course, I'm making money. What's it to you?"

"I need borrow some of it," Sten said.

"Borrow? How much?"

"A hundred grand ought to do it."

Ida exploded. "A hundred clottin' grand? Are you nuts? Stoned? Kidnapped? What?"

"I have a vital need to lay a bet on a Xypaca fight," Sten said.

Ida was scornful. "Riiiigggghhhhtttt!" she said. Then: "What the clot do you know about Xypacas?" she demanded.

"You'd be surprised," Sten said.

"Give me a clottin' break," Ida said. "They're like chicken fights on steroids. Nobody, but nobody, can figure the odds on those little scrotes. They're too skitzy."

"Nevertheless," Sten said. "I need to make this bet."

"What if you're wrong?" Ida asked. "What if you lose? How are you going to pay me back?"

"It's for a mission," Sten said. "A legitimate Mantis expense. They'll be obligated to cover our losses."

"So, you have Mahoney's approval, do you?" Ida said.

"Not exactly," Sten said. "But he's going to love us when he finds out. Maybe even let us off these interminable babysitting tours."

Silence. Ida was as frustrated and bored as the rest of them. Maybe even more so. For a Rom to be cut out of the main action for all these months was beyond maddening.

Finally, she said. "Okay. I'll transfer the credits to your account. But it's against my better judgment."

"I understand," Sten said.

But before he could key off, she asked, "Say, Sten? There wouldn't be a woman involved in this, would there?"

"That's a clotting insult," Sten said. "How dare you suggest that I'm ruled by my gonads?"

"I knew it," Ida chortled. And then she was gone.

* * * *

While Alex went about his dirty work, Sten moved through the fight crowd until he was close enough to Venatora to draw the attention of her Zabanya guardswomen.

As he grew nearer, the guardswomen nudged one another. Fierce glares and muscle flexing followed as they blew themselves up like so many two-legged puff fish to present a fortress of flesh and bone.

He ignored the women. Instead he studied the two Xypacas being presented to the crowd by the Fightmaster. She held a cage gripped in each claw, two pairs of eyestalks wiggling excitedly as she showed off her fierce charges.

Sten couldn't hear the Fightmaster's pitch over the roar of the crowd and the blood-curdling shrieks of the Xypacas, who were mad to fight. But she was obviously pointing out each beast's fighting credentials and breeding

The creatures were nearly identical in size and ferocity, so there was no apparent advantage of one over the other.

Drawing on his father's impromptu cage lessons, Sten carefully studied them, looking for weaknesses and strengths.

It was then that he spotted what looked like a deformed talon in the back claw of one of the Xypacas—a half white, half black talon, as though some old injury had cut off its blood supply. Oddsmakers would mark the talon as a slight handicap. He'd heard something about that kind of claw from his father, though....

He turned his attention to the other Xypaca. A piece of its tail had been chomped off in a previous fight. Not an obvious problem, although it might affect balance in the lightning-fast match.

Sten made his choice, then very casually...very deliberately... turned to see what Venatora had in mind.

The Zabanya guards didn't appreciate his attention and went back to muscle displays, while loudly cracking their necks and knuckles.

That irritated Venatora and she snapped at them. They ducked their heads and grumbled, but kept their eyes fixed on Sten.

Meanwhile, with an imperious gesture, their boss caught the attention of the Oddsmaster. She pointed at the Xypaca with the chomped on tail and raised a questioning hand.

The Oddsmaster signaled: It was the favorite—barely. Venatora nodded, no doubt thinking several others had spotted the blackened talon deformity on the other beast.

She signaled her wager: two thousand credits, then turned away. As she did so Sten caught her eye, held it, then shook his head, as if disappointed in her decision.

Then he signaled his wager to the Oddsmaster: two thousand credits on the Xypaca with the black talon. He turned back to Venatora, who had watched his every move.

Sten shrugged, smiled and gifted her with another sad shake of the head.

Venatora's lips tightened. Her eyes glittered. Was she angry? Or challenged?

Sten pointed at her, then tapped his chest. Raised a questioning hand. *Side bet?*

Venatora looked interested. She signaled, back: *Five thousand credits?*

Sten nodded and mouthed the words, "You're on."

They signaled their intent to the Oddsmaster, who banked their credits and escrowed their bets.

Then the Xypacas were freed from their cages. With ear-piercing shrieks, they closed on one another so fast that even Sten— who knew what to expect—experienced the Xypaca rush: breath suddenly sticking in his throat, heart jumping, and for a split second he felt like he was in that fight.

His father had warned him about the effect. It was the reason, he said, that Xypaca bouts were so addictive. All the white hot fight-or-flight juices spurted through your body, and you felt like you was in the middle of that ripping, biting, clawing fighting ring.

Sten pulled back from the excitement. Calmed himself until he could coolly judge the action. As expected, Chomp Tail was off balance. A claw strike missed at a crucial moment, almost ending the fight there. But, also as expected, Black Talon favored his rear claw, holding back, instead of taking immediate advantage of his enemy's clumsiness.

Chomp Tail, however, did not lack carnivore cunning. She'd

spotted the defect early on, and whenever she got the chance, she went after that side, attacking again and again and again. Knowing that in less than a minute the claw would be useless and she'd sink her fangs into her enemy's throat, while all four of her claws raked its chest and belly. Death would soon follow.

One look at Venatora and Sten could see that her eyes were ablaze with Xypaca madness. Muscles in her arms and hands and taut abdomen reflexively jumping in sympathy as her Xypaca pressed the attack—going for that claw, going for that claw.

If she had looked closer at her enemy she might have seen what was coming. Because that black talon was only half black: rear section black, and apparently dead, front section a healthy white.

But even if she had spotted it, she'd have to know about the rare Xypacas with half-black talons.

Years before Sten's father had told him about this rare mutation.

He'd said, "Son, if you should ever see a Xypaca with a half-black talon, you get your hands on every credit you can beg, borrow or thump somebody out of, and you bet it all on that Xypaca." He shook his head, marveling at that imagined bet. "Why, you'd win so much money—I mean take-this-contract-and-shove-it money, boy, if you get my meaning." A sigh. "Never seen one myself, but if I ever do...if I ever do..."

"But Dad," Sten said, "you didn't say how come."

"How come what, son?"

"How come a Half-Black can't lose?"

"Why, the poison, son, the poison."

"What poison."

"That black part isn't dead, son. It's a poison sac. And it's not just any old poison. It hits like a lighting strike... *Boom!* You're a dead 'un."

Sten was snatched back from that memory as Chomp Tail went for it big time, extending herself almost full length to get at her enemy's weakest point.

Just what the Half-Black was waiting for.

A flick of the back claw, and the deadly talon pierced Chomp Tail's neck. Injecting the poison.

And, just as Sten's father had said, it was as if Chomp Tail had been struck by lightning. Her whole body jolted, went rigid, and then she was dead.

The winners roared, the losers moaned—a few shouting that the fix was in. But that wasn't going anywhere with officials.

Dead was clearly dead.

Sten turned to see the expected look of fury on Venatora's beautiful face. Eyes boiling. Nostrils flaring. Lush lips parted to reveal her sharp white teeth.

Now, if he played his cards just right…

Sten caught Venatora's attention, smiled, then gave her a half bow. This seemed to enraged her even more.

Until Sten flashed another signal: Again?

She blinked. Took a step back. Then smiled the most delicious smile Sten had ever enjoyed.

She signaled back: *Again.*

Sten motioned: *When?*

She signaled, mouthing the words: "Feature match."

Sten sent a query: *How much?*

Venatora fixed him with smile of marvelous mystery, eyes taunting, daring.

And she signaled: *100,000 credits?*

She looked surprised when Sten instantly signaled back: *Deal.*

CHAPTER EIGHT

SINKING THE HOOK

The feature match was called, and two terrified minders carried out the cage of the Scarlet Xypaca, who raged and tore at the bars with fang and claw.

Hurriedly they set her down and jumped away.

A moment later, another pair of minders emerged carrying a second cage, which they gingerly bore to the opposite side of the ring.

The cage contained the green Xypaca, who was smaller but no less fierce. She attacked her cage, crazy to get at the scarlet enemy.

Sten looked over at Venatora. Perspiration glistened on her ebony skin, and her body trembled with excitement. The full force of Xypaca fever was upon her.

Meanwhile her female entourage was so stirred by the boss's mood they could barely contain themselves. Pacing about, growling indiscriminately at anyone who dared to come close, clenching their fists and flexing their muscles, aching for a fight.

Venatora turned to look at Sten. She sneered at him, as if saying, *You just wait and see, you little piece of drakh. You just wait and see.*

Sten blew her a kiss. He turned away as if he hadn't a care in the Empire. Although he had to push away the strange aura of eroticism emanating from her like an odorless perfume that enveloped him in warm blanket of lust.

Even so, he didn't need eyes in the back of his head to know she was ready to explode at his casual manner.

The Fightmaster called for action. The cage gates swung open. The crowd roared. The green Xypaca hopped out. On the other side of the ring, the Scarlet Fury exited her cage, shrieking a challenge.

The Green Xypaca returned the shriek.

And charged.

The Scarlet Fury took half a step forward, then stopped. Hunched over. Abdomen squeezing in and out. Jaws gaping.

Choking.

Choking.

Like cat trying to rid itself of a hairball.

Then the beast spewed an enormous mound of red, quivering jelly-like soy steak. And it spewed and spewed and spewed.

Until the green Xypaca fell upon it and tore off its head.

Sten turned away from the scene and casually walked toward Venatora, wearing his best Cheshire grin. The closer he came, the angrier she became, and the angrier she became, the more her guards were affected.

By the time Sten reached her they were ready to swarm him and tear him to pieces. She raised a hand, stopping them, but not calming them. If that was even possible. Their blood was well past simmer.

Venatora spoke. "Is that your work?" she demanded, pointing at the ring, where, no doubt, the victor was feeding on the late Scarlet Fury.

Sten looked hurt. Hand on breast. *Me?*

Then he said, "They didn't tell me you were a sore loser."

Venatora said, "It looks to me like the fix was in."

"Don't tell me you're going to protest the fight," Sten said. "Renege on the bet."

She didn't like that one bit. Almost blew. But then she remembered her gambler's pride and pulled back. She looked him up and down, then said:

"Are you the law?"

Sten laughed. "I'm just a poor soldier on leave."

Venatora scoffed. "A soldier so poor he can wager one hundred thousand credits? Somehow…" She let the rest trail off.

Sten said, "I have a sideline."

"And that would be?"

"I sell things?"

"What sort of things?"

"Information, mainly."

"And who do you sell this information to?"

Another Cheshire grin. "To people like you."

Venatora covered her surprise. But couldn't help a little blush of pleasure. She was starting to enjoy this game.

"And who might I be?"

"A pirate," Sten said.

Venatora touched her breast with slender fingertips, mimicking Sten. "Me? A pirate?"

"Not just a pirate," Sten said. He motioned at her bodyguards, who flinched and growled. "But a pirate queen."

Venatora barked laughter. "I'm no queen," she said. "Just a boss lady."

"Then it's settled," Sten said. "You're a boss lady pirate. Just the kind I like to meet."

Venatora looked him over. Light shone in her eyes. She seemed to approve of what she saw.

"Maybe we can do business someday," she said. "When you have something of value for sale."

Then, catching Sten by surprise, she abruptly motioned to her guardswomen and started away.

He tried to follow, but they blocked him.

"Wait," Sten called after her. "How can I get in touch with you?"

"Don't worry," she called back. "When you have something I want, I'll know how to find you."

Sten laughed. The woman was a delight. Then the laugh turned to a scowl as she vanished into the gaming room crowd.

He suddenly felt let down. Chilled. As if someone had turned off the hot water in the fresher. The erotic atmosphere that surrounded Venatora was gone.

Alex rejoined him. Caught his mood. Slapped him on the back.

"Come on, wee Sten," he said. "There's girls everywhere, in case you hadn't noticed."

Then he fetched mugs of Stregg off a passing barbot and handed one to Sten, who drained the mug and grabbed another.

Once again the mood restoratives did wonders. Sten saw a particularly attractive Joygirl giving him the eye and smiled. Encouraged, she started toward him.

But then a hulking security bot shouldered its way onto the scene, blocking her path. It was humanoid in shape, half again larger than a man, made of mottled steel, with an oversized face sporting a single, glowing red eye.

That eye fixed itself on Sten. The bot raised a commanding hand, and beckoned with a long, metal finger.

"Lieutenant Sten," it rumbled. "Come."

The eye moved to Alex. Again, the beckoning finger beckoned. "Sergeant Kilgour," the bot growled. "You come too."

The bot started away, the crowd scurrying out of its path. Sten and Alex did not immediately follow."

"What do you want?" Sten shouted after it. "What's going on?"

The answer came rumbling back: "Mahoney! Mahoney say come!"

Sten and Alex looked at one another. What the clot?

"Doesn't Mahoney know we're on leave?" Sten said, getting a little hot.

"'Course he does," Alex said.

From out of the crowd came the security bot's demanding voice: "Come."

Sten sighed. "Best not keep the General waiting," he said.

CHAPTER NINE

ORDERS FROM ON HIGH

"Venatora is a splicer," Mahoney said. "One of the oddest forms of that breed—and I use the term very loosely—that I've ever encountered."

They were in a dark, empty utility room deep in the bowels of Rec Area 477. The walls of the room were black with mold, and Mahoney's wavering holo image floated ghostlike above the floor.

He made snipping motions with two fingers. "Bits of one species joined with another. In her case, a little Himmenops, a lot of human. And a large dollop of something extra that turned her into a Himmenops queen."

"It's more than a dollop," Sten said. "And it doesn't just work on Himmenops."

Alex grinned at this. "Aye, the wee lieutenant was quite taken with the bonny lass, sir," Alex said. He put a hand over his heart, a sure sign that a Bobby Burns poem was coming on: "Had we ne'er lov'd sae kindly/ Had we ne'er lov'd sae blindly…"

Sten wanted to tell him to stifle it, but with the boss of the Mantis Section present, all he could do was glare.

Mahoney chuckled. "From what Rykor's operative reported," he said, "your lust quotient was off the charts."

Rykor was the head of Mercury Corps Psy-Ops and it was hardly surprising that she had an operative or three on the premises. Probably the Joygirl Sten had his eye on before being summoned.

"I admit Venatora got to me, General," Sten said, knowing full well this an understatement to the extreme. In reality, the affect she had on him was intoxicating. "But I maintained control through the whole operation, sir. I had the upper hand the entire time."

"Our reading exactly," Mahoney said. "But next time you

meet, she'll have your measure."

Sten's heart gave an involuntary bump. "Meet, sir?"

Alex said, "Ah think th' General's tellin' us, laddie, 'at we hae a wee mission tae perf'rm."

Sten was still young enough and new enough to the Mantis game to feel manipulated. "You mean this whole thing was a setup, sir?" he said. "The leave? The choice of this hellhole for a vacation spa? All for me to meet Venatora?"

Mahoney shrugged. "We didn't expect the Xypaca business," he said. "That was just pure dumb luck. But Rykor predicted you would be irresistibly drawn to her."

Sten frowned. "How could Rykor—"

Mahoney cut him off with a raised hand. "You'll have to ask her," he said. "It's a doctor/patient thing."

Rykor, the walrus-like being with an oh-so-elegant mind, had been one of Sten's keenest mentors from the start and had done a great deal to heal the wounds left by the loss of his family on Vulcan.

Sten sighed. He was whipped.

"What's the operation, sir?" he asked.

"Mutiny," Mahoney said.

Sten gawped in astonishment. As did Alex and Ida. Even Doc twitched—momentarily ruining his mask of supreme serenity.

Mutiny was unheard of in the Imperial Navy. The penalty for mutiny was death. And anyone associated with the mutiny—no matter how official the capacity—was in danger of having a permanent black mark on his record.

"Not to worry, lads," Mahoney said, as if reading their thoughts. "You'll get nothing but kudos for this. There'll be no blowback, or black marks on your personnel file."

Sten grimaced. "You mean as long as we are successful, sir," he said.

Mahoney waved an impatient hand. That went without saying. In the shadow world of Mantis Section, winning was the only option.

He went on to outline the situation. The crew of a merchant escort ship had mutinied. Stealing a fortune in Imperium X in the process. Moreover, the mutineers were using the Imperium X as a bargaining chip. They were demanding a fortune in credits, and either amnesty from prosecution if the Emperor made the highest bid, or asylum in the pirate world if Venatora won.

"The boss wants this handled as quietly as possible," Mahoney said. "No battleships. No military posturing or noise of any kind." He shrugged. "Besides, the pirates are dug in too deep to get at easily. One false move on our part will drive the mutineers right into Venatora's more than willing arms."

"Why hasn't anyone done anything about her before?" Sten asked.

"We should have taken care of this problem long ago," Mahoney admitted. "But the whole Imperium X boom caught us flat-footed. And now Venatora and the other pirates have the Possnet Sector so fortified that the cost in money and blood to root them out will be an embarrassment to the Emperor. An embarrassment that couldn't come at a worse time."

Sten and Alex had heard backchannel rumors that the Emperor was engaged in delicate negotiations with the Tahn—a formidable ultra-warlike race—had been attracting allies to their cause at an alarming rate. So far, the Emperor had maintained the upper hand, skillfully shoring up his side while quietly undermining the Tahn.

Of course, this whole mutiny business, along with the theft of a space-train load of Imperium X, would be portrayed by his enemies as yet another sign of weakness. Not only was security lacking, with criminal enterprises allowed to go on unchecked, but the Emperor's own forces—sworn to uphold his law—dared to defy him.

The Tahn would say this was proof aplenty that the Empire was old and creaky and in desperate need of new ideas and new leadership.

Which the Tahn would magnanimously offer to provide.

Sten said, "So, let me get this straight, General. You want us—a combat team—to suddenly become diplomats and negotiate on behalf of the Empire."

"Ne'er fear, young Sten," Alex said. "Our wee General's a magician of th' highest order. Waves his magic wand an'—poof!— four Mantis killers turn intae nice, gentle tea-drinkin' legates."

Ida laughed. "Can you all see me in a ball gown," she said. "dancing the night away with princes and presidents at some gala palace soirée?"

Doc broke in. "I suspect the General is more interested in our killing skills than our diplomatic abilities."

"That's certainly been taken into consideration," Mahoney said dryly. "And we have planned accordingly."

"A couple of observations, sir," Sten said. "First, to put on a good show we'll need a decent looking ship. Nothing too fancy. The *Storm* just won't do. She would look out of place here in the boonies. We have to show up in something that is at least the equal to their ship. But not loaded down with so much armament that it would make them soak their jocks."

"Their ship is the *Flame*," Mahoney said. "Light cruiser. Radoslaw class."

"Do we have anything similar on hand?" Sten asked.

"As it happens," Mahoney said, "The *Flame*'s sister ship—the *Jo'l Cash*—is being refitted at the same yard where they're working on the *Storm*. It's identical in looks and weaponry."

"Perfect, sir," Sten said. "What about rank? They're not going to believe the Emperor is serious about negotiating if he sends a mere lieutenant. On the other hand, I'm too young to have advanced much higher."

Mahoney nodded. "Not a problem, lad," he said. "We'll make you a flag lieutenant. Or, better yet, a captain. Nephew to Admiral Mik Ledoh."

Alex laughed. "Nepotism. Thae's th' ticket, sir," he said. "Every workin' cheil knows th' boss's bairn gits the poshest job."

Mahoney fell silent. Sten could tell that he was holding something back.

"What is it, sir?" he prodded. "If this is going to work, we have to know everything."

Mahoney sighed. And told him the rest. Sten's outraged response was a surprise to the old spymaster.

"Rescue Gregor?" he said, voice shaking with anger. "Begging your pardon, sir, but has everyone on Prime lost their clotting minds?"

"From your reaction, Lieutenant," Mahoney said, "would I be wrong in thinking that you know Captain Gregor?"

"Know and loathe him, sir," Sten said. "He was the biggest, most dangerous screwup in Guard training. Nearly got more than one of us injured, or even killed. And he's a spoiled little bastard.

Always bragging about how rich and important his father is. Acted like he was better than everyone else. Shirked his work and dumped it on others. Everybody hated him."

"Maybe somebody shoolda given heem a boot in th' bollocks," Alex said.

"Gregor did get the boot," Sten said. "Right out of the Guard."

He looked at Mahoney, a glint of accusation in his eyes. "Well sir, seems they let his father buy Gregor's way back in. Not only that, they gave him rank. Responsibility. And he screwed it up so much that he drove one hundred and twenty nine of our own people so far around the bend that they mutinied."

"You're forgetting they also stole all that Imperium X," Mahoney said dryly. "A bad apple skipper wasn't their only motivation. Greed obviously had something to do with it."

"Th' wee General has a point, lad," Alex said. "Mebbe this Gregor is a screwup ay th' first order. But I'll wager a black-hearted pirate whispered in their shell-likes, promisin' grand fortunes fur aw."

"Sergeant Kilgour is spot on," Mahoney said. "We have intelligence that several crew members were contacted by Venatora's people. A deal was obviously made. At the opportune time, the crew would mutiny, seize the cargo, and live like royalty the rest of their days."

"But that's not exactly what happened, is it, sir?" Sten said.

Mahoney sighed. "No, it didn't," he said. "The crew mutinied on schedule, but apparently not all of them agreed with their leaders."

"Let me guess, sir," Alex broke in. "They're sayin' they nae be traitors, but jist honest Guardsbeings who hae bin badly used by their officers."

"So, they're frozen in indecision, right sir?" Sten said. "They got their blood up, but now a large minority of them are sorry. And they are looking for a way out."

"All we have to do," Mahoney said, "is beat Venatora's price."

"And amnesty, sir," Sten said. "You said they wanted amnesty."

"That I did," Mahoney said. "And you can offer it to them."

A long silence followed. As Sten and the others thought this through, Mahoney could see doubt written on all of their faces.

Finally, Sten said, "So, we'll be giving them my word, sir?"

Sten ventured. "About the amnesty?"

"You will," Mahoney said.

"They'll get the ransom money, then go free," Sten pressed. "That's what we'll be saying, right?"

"Yes," Mahoney said. "That's exactly what you should say. And you should also swear them to secrecy. Not a word of this incident can get out. If it does, the amnesty is off. And they'll all be given fair trial. And then shot."

"So as not to encourage similar incidents, right, sir?" Sten said—rather tentatively. Suspicion prickled the back of his neck.

"Exactly," Mahoney said. "After they agree, you just have to give us a whistle and I'll have a task force near at hand to take charge."

Sten thought a minute, then said, "What about Venatora, sir?" he asked. "She's not just going to stand by and let all this happen without interfering."

"I don't expect she will," Mahoney said.

"So what should we do about her, sir?" he asked. "What are your orders?"

"The Emperor wants her dead," Mahoney said. "Just as dead as she can be."

Mahoney's holo image started to waver, then just before it blinked out, Ian leaned in and the image steadied.

"Don't forget Gregor," Mahoney said. "His daddy wants him back."

And then he was gone.

"Clot Gregor," Sten said. "And clot his daddy, too."

CHAPTER TEN

GREGOR

Gregor stared morosely at the dinner plate. It was divided into three sections. Drakh-brown glop with lumps the size of marbles filled the largest section.

This was the entrée. He'd never had the nerve to ask what the lumps were.

More glop formed a mound in the second section—but it was grayish green with yellow streaks and had the consistency of garbage-pail slime.

This was the starch.

The third section contained the alleged sweet. It was purplish glop, with orange spots.

He sighed and with great reluctance jabbed a plas spoon into the brown glop. Raised it to his lips, trying not to notice the long, snot-like strings stretching between spoon and plate.

Gregor got ready. The trick was not to breathe. He stuck the spoon into his mouth—face contorting at the taste—and then he forced himself to swallow, half gagging and choking as he got it down.

He let his breath out in whoosh, grabbed a mug of badly-recycled water, and drank it down, doing his damndest to dilute the disgusting taste.

The water was almost as bad as the brown glop and for a moment he thought the battle was lost and nearly vomited. By sheer force of will he kept it down. Then he slumped back in his chair, gathering the courage and strength to start on the starchy slime.

Gregor began by cursing the traitorous crew members in general and their back-stabbing ringleaders in particular for humiliating him so. He was their *Captain*, by God. A being they had sworn to obey when they joined the Emperor's Merchant Service. It was as solemn an oath as any Imperial sailor made.

Well, almost as solemn. They weren't really professionals. Only quasi-military, as some of his old prep-school chums cruelly reminded him when they got together at their fathers' clubs. But only a few dared say it to his face. And then only if they were drunk enough to forget just how important his old man was.

His dad, Lord Wichman, was not only the president and CEO of Wichman XII, the most exclusive resort planet in the Empire, but he had been presented at court, was a board member on a dozen or more vital businesses and industries, and was a regular honored guest at the annual Empire Day festivities at Arundel Castle.

When Gregor was a lad, he'd actually sat in the same box as the Eternal Emperor. During one performance an aerialist had slipped and fell thirty feet, hitting the ground so hard it looked like she bounced.

It was one of the funniest things Gregor had ever seen—the young woman's arms flailing, the gaping fish-like look on her face, emitting hilarious squeaky noises, topped off by the humorous double bounce when she hit the ground.

Naturally, he'd laughed, and then he heard someone snort and he turned to see that the Emperor was looking at him. And he was smiling. Well, it was sort of a smile. On bad nights—and there had been many since he washed out of the Guard several years before—it seemed to him that the smile looked more like a grimace of disgust.

But when he woke with the cold sweats, he calmed himself by thinking that at the worst it was merely the look of royal indigestion.

Remembering the self-doubt, Gregor's stomach roiled, and he pushed the plate of three glops away. Please, God, why did he have to eat this swill? There was plenty of good food in his private locker—seized by the mutineers, no doubt.

Zheng and the others were probably enjoying his larder this very minute. Laughing at him all the while. All those delicacies: real beef steak, lobster, caviar, pâté, foie gras, plus all those special breads and cheeses and other gourmet treats. Washed down with fine wines and champagne.

Instead, they were feeding him the barest minimum. Contractually, merchantmen were entitled to three BCM (Basic Crew Meal) containers a day, totaling 1,800 calories for humans, with different nutritional requirements for ETs.

Gregor was a little over two meters in height, and before starvation had been forced on him, he weighed a slightly chubby 88 kilos. He didn't know how much he weighed now, but there was no chub at all on his frame, and his uniform hung off him like a clown suit.

Of course, no one in their right mind would eat this garbage, much less try to subsist on it. Which is why Gregor, who considered himself an enlightened captain, had instituted a generous program with special menus for a small percentage of the crew members' wages.

Naturally he made a profit, but his father had taught him that profit was as essential to life as clean air—which was another little side business Gregor had going.

For a fair price, sweet-smelling air—instead of the oily recycled shipboard atmosphere—could be had by turning a nozzle above each being's bunk.

It was sweet and cool and made for easy sleep. Of course, if a being wasn't frugal and was burdened with family responsibilities, they obviously couldn't afford that inexpensive luxury and nothing but foul air would be emitted when the nozzle was turned.

But that was to be expected. Fair was fair. After all, Gregor wasn't in the charity business. And he worked hard to supplement his wages and the allowance his father regularly banked for him. He constantly, and assiduously, searched for new ways to turn a profit.

Skimming and reselling supplies, buying refurbished equipment and clothing for the crew and pocketing the difference, as well as selling favorable shifts and appointments whenever the opportunity arose. And charging for little things, like emergency leave to visit ailing family members.

It wasn't much, but when it came to maintaining a ship and crew of 129, as well as a 125-kilometer-long space-train, even a small percentage made a handsome sum when the mission ended.

And if a crew member made so bold as to complain, Gregor heaped on enough demerits so they could never go on leave and spread these subversive objections to others.

Gregor repositioned the dish of three glops. He had to eat,

damn it. The mutiny was already over a month old; no telling when the ordeal would end. He had to keep his strength up. His wits keen. And keep a constantly lookout for anything that might aid his chances of survival.

Gingerly, he stabbed the spoon into the purple blob with orange stripes. As a sweet it would surely have more calories, so he might not have to eat as much.

He held his breath.

Took a bite.

Then vomited his guts on the floor.

He was bent over heaving when the cabin door banged open. There was silence. Then laughter. He looked up to see Zheng's gloating face.

Zheng was short and squat and had a habit of constantly licking his lips with a shockingly pink tongue. Not unlike a toad, Gregor thought.

Behind him was Rual, a tall, skeletal, vaguely humanoid female of indeterminate age. She had a long, stern face with large, black unblinking eyes. Gregor had never seen her smile, much less laugh.

"Gutt damn! Vhat a filthy miststuck you be, Gregor," Zheng said. "Drakh for brains, also you have."

He glanced over his shoulder at Rual. "I think maybe Poppa had to pay somebody big credits to make him captain."

Rual measured him with cold eyes. Gregor shivered. "If we can't get a deal with the Emperor," she said, "I want to be the one who cuts his throat."

Before Zheng could answer, someone else came forward. It was Shaklin. A tall, handsome young man with dark skin, beaded dreadlocks, and misty brown eyes that always seemed as if they were searching for things no one else could see.

"Zheng, you swore there would be no killing," he said, elbowing Rual aside. "Otherwise, my teammates and I would have never agreed to join you."

Shaklin was a self-proclaimed bishop of the Church of the Universal Location, a religion Gregor had never heard of before. More importantly, he and his team of nineteen beings came from a race of tribal navigators who had obsessively roamed their home planet, mapping every conceivable position, from the molten interior to the upper atmosphere and eventually on to uttermost space. In short, they were the only beings aboard the *Flame* who could safely navigate from one place to next. They were also the ace up Zheng's sleeve. If boarders threatened the ship, Shaklin and his team could swiftly plot a series of jumps so complicated they would be impossible to follow.

Rual clearly wasn't happy with Shaklin's interference. Her hand went to the haft of the long knife sheathed in her belt.

"If we take Venatora's deal," she said, "we won't need Gregor—or you. So back the clot off, holy man."

Then she turned to Gregor. "In fact," she said, "I have a mind to kill the scrote right now. To slice his lying throat from ear to ear."

As she advanced on him, Gregor felt sudden wetness at his crotch.

"Please," he squeaked to the others. "Please!"

CHAPTER ELEVEN

A MATTER OF PROFIT

Gregor shrank back in his bunk as Rual came for him, pulling the long knife from her belt.

But then to his enormous relief Shaklin stepped between them, blocking her.

A nasty grin creased Rual's face. "Don't mind doing you first, Holy Man," she said. "You and your teammates are always acting like you're better than the rest of us."

"Now, now," Zheng broke in. "We here all be shipmates. Very rich shipmates, soon to be. Quarrel, we must not."

He put a restraining hand on Rual's knife arm. "Shaklin, a good man is he," Zheng said in his most soothing voice. "In his head, he lives. In his church, he lives. Beings, all equal, he believes."

Gregor could see the war going on in Rual's face. She badly wanted to kill Gregor and didn't give a damn one way or another if Shaklin had to go first. Whether Shaklin was a good man or not had no bearing on what was going to happen next. But by sheer force of will, the canny Zheng was getting a far more important message across. Without Shaklin and his crew the whole enterprise would fail and they'd all soon be against the wall facing an Imperial firing squad.

Rual sighed and stepped away, sheathing her blade. Now Zheng turned to Shaklin, who was clearly furious at being threatened. Zheng gave Shaklin's shoulder a comradely squeeze.

"Mind not our Rual's temper," he said. "Sometimes, too hot it becomes."

Rual's face reddened and Zheng hastily added, "And good reason for this temper, she has." He indicated Gregor. "Much suffering, this man has caused our Rual."

Gregor snorted. This was too much.

"It's not my fault she's a gambling addict," Gregor said. "I put in that gaming area in the Rec Room for the entertainment of the crew. And at my own expense, I might add."

He pointed an accusing finger at Rual. "She's in there every minute off shift dumping credits into the machines. Why, I even caught her in there gaming during work hours. Having her fun on company time."

Fury once again overtook Rual. Drawing her knife, she pushed past the other two men and would have buried it hilt deep into Gregor's chest if Shaklin hadn't grabbed her wrist and spun her around.

While Gregor cowered in his bunk, Rual struggled, screaming curses and threats. She nearly broke away. But then Zheng jumped in and helped Shaklin disarm her.

Rual collapsed, shedding bitter tears. "Gone, gone," she moaned. "Every credit I had in savings. My pension fund. I even took money from my own family."

She jabbed an accusing finger at Gregor. "The machines are rigged," she said. "The concessionaire at the last port told me so himself. He was chuffed because the captain made him pull his machines—machines with fair odds approved by the company—and installed his own."

Frightened as he was, Gregor couldn't help but feel a flash of pride. It had been one of his cleverest moves. Not only had he fixed the odds so they were more favorable to the House—meaning himself—but he'd installed a special program that targeted certain individuals.

It sussed out weak-willed scrotes like Rual and played them like a cat toying with its prey. Letting them win a few rounds—sometimes even for large sums of money. Then, *wham!* The gaming fist would come slamming down. The mark would be taken for every credit he possessed, and then a loan program would pop up, offering usurious interest rates for immediate gratification. And when that was gone, the hacked names and contact numbers of friends and relatives would appear, and the mark would be enticed to contact them immediately for loans.

The program even offered suggestions the mark could use to wheedle money from those who hesitated. A fictitious daughter suffering from an equally fictitious malady. Or, the mark might be encouraged to say the child had been kidnapped, possibly even injured.

The wheedling possibilities were endless.

It wasn't Gregor's fault that Rual and her ilk were all such willing liars. Such low class beings that they'd bankrupt their own loved ones to feed their filthy habits. They were born victims and would more than likely die victims.

He shook his head in disgust. "Not my fault," he whispered.

To his horror, it seemed that Rual had only been shamming. Waiting for her chance. As the others gaped at Gregor for speaking so foolishly, she jumped for him.

Somehow the knife was in her hand again, the sharp edge gleaming in the cabin light.

The blade swung, and Gregor screamed in pain as the it slashed across his chest. Hot blood spilling.

Once again, the blade slashed at him, but somehow Shaklin got there in time and grabbed Rual's wrist.

Then Zheng stepped in, embracing Rual. The fury drained away, and she collapsed into his arms, weeping and sobbing that she was sorry, so sorry.

And Zheng was saying, "Never mind. Never mind. Soon, put right all will be. More credits than dreams you will ever have. And fixed, your family will be. Proud of you again, they will be."

Meanwhile, Shaklin had rustled up a first aid kit. Skillfully, he stripped off Gregor's shirt and dabbed the wound with cotton swatches.

"It's not so bad," he said. "Maybe only six or seven staples will do the job."

Gregor gasped as she poured a stinging liquid into his wound. Then he was groaning in pain as she got out the medical stapler and hit him six, then seven, then eight times.

Tears streamed down Gregor's face. "You could have used the anesthetic," he said, pointing at the slender cylinder next to the bandages. "It's there in plain sight."

Shaklin snorted derision. "You're lucky I wasn't holding the knife," he said. "If anyone has the right to take your life it's me." A single tear ran down his cheek. "You are the reason Pegatha was taken from us."

Desperate, Gregor grabbed the cylinder and pressed it next to the wound. There was a slight sting and then the pain vanished. Gregor sank back in his bunk, drawing in deep breaths to regain a modicum of control.

And with control came a feeling of bitter resentment. Shaklin's remark had been so unfair. The accusation as false as it was scurrilous. It wasn't his fault Shaklin's mate had died. An airlock malfunction. She just happened to be in the wrong place at the wrong time.

True, a port maintenance inspector had spotted the faulty airlock seal. But replacing it would have put Gregor so far behind schedule that it endangered his mission bonus.

Besides, the inspector said it wasn't that serious and was happy to sign off on the airlock—plus all the *Flame*'s other maintenance difficulties—for a hefty fee. Well, not so hefty that Gregor couldn't expect a handsome profit when he received his well-deserved bonus.

Gregor had been taught by his father, Lord Wichman, that profit was life's Holy Grail. And for profit, there will always be risk. Sometimes risk might cause discomfort for a few beings. But that was the price one must be willing to pay for success.

It briefly occurred to Gregor that Shaklin and the other mutineers might be presently engaged in just that sort of risk taking. Betting their lives against the chance of great profit.

Then another thought occurred to him and he couldn't help but smile.

And then someone slapped him hard across the face. He reeled back, raising a hand against another blow.

"What was that for?" he whined.

"Smiling, you were," Zheng said. It was he who had delivered the blow. "Why smile, you?"

"Oh… Oh… It was nothing," Gregor said. "Just the anesthetic. Feeling a little woozy."

And he bit his lip against another reflexive smile. He had just figured out how he might turn all this misery into a pot of gold.

He looked up at Zheng. "Have you started negotiations with the Empire yet?"

Zheng was non committal. "Spoken to them, we have," he said.

In other words—a big clotting, "No."

"Well, before you get to far along," Gregor said, "I hope you'll consult with me."

Rual snorted. "Why would we do that?"

"Because with my father's influence," Gregor said, "I can help you get a much better deal."

"We've already got an offer from Venatora," Rual said. "I say we just take it and be done with the whole business. Every day we delay, the more dangerous it becomes."

"But what if I can get you more?" Gregor said. "A whole clot of a lot more."

Silence fell upon the room. Zheng's pink tongue flashed out to lick his lips. There was a definite glitter in Rual's eyes.

Gregor looked at Shaklin. Other than fingering his dreadlocks, the man showed no emotion whatsoever. He'd sworn to everyone in the cabin that he opposed killing Gregor. So revenge wasn't his motive. And money? As impossible as that seemed to someone like Gregor, riches apparently held no great attraction to Shaklin.

So what was it that Shaklin wanted?

Suddenly the tall black man straightened and turned to go. "It's time for the Nav check," he said and hurriedly left the cabin.

"A Nav check?" Rual said. "What the clotting big deal? We've been—mas o menos—in the same place for the last month. What's to check?"

"If happy it makes him," Zheng said, "Care, I do not." He turned to Gregor. "Now, little cheena," he said. "More, I want to know about your father."

And so Gregor told him more, only needing to exaggerate a little. His father was that important.

But in the back of his mind he kept worrying over the Shaklin conundrum.

If money wasn't his object, what else could it be?

Hard as he tried, Gregor couldn't come up with a thing. What the clot could be more important than money?

CHAPTER TWELVE

THE CORPSES IN THE TOOLROOM

Kilgour said, "I cannae bloody see."

Stifling a groan, Sten turned his head in the direction of Alex's voice. He felt dizzy. Confused.

With great difficulty, he pondered Kilgour's dilemma.

Finally, all he could think to say was: "Have you tried opening your eyes?"

He sensed movement. A large body shifting. Joints cracking. Then: "Ooch!"

"What's wrong?"

"Stuck a bloody finger in me peeper." A pause, then, "Who shut off the clottin' lights?"

Sten laughed and was immediately sorry. His body felt like it had been hit with a planet buster. He considered Alex's question a moment, then remembered.

"That would be me," he said. "When they jumped us, I just had time enough to cut a handy power cable."

Even though he couldn't see his friend's face, Sten sensed confusion easily equal to his own.

"When *who* jumped us?" Kilgour said. "Last thin' Ah remember is arguin' aboot who should drive the gravsled."

"Then you don't remember Mahoney?" Sten asked.

Another long pause. Finally: "Oh, aye. Th' wee General. We were supposed tae meet up fur orders. Somethin' abit some mutineers."

"We had the meeting," Sten said, recalling same. "And we got our orders."

Alex sighed. "Ah don't quite recollect. Are we supposed tae kill th' puir buggers? If so, we've got tae catch 'em first."

Sten said, "We weren't supposed to kill anybody. Not yet, at any rate. This was just supposed to be a recon job. Meet a barkeep. Get some intel. Maybe lay a trap."

Another groan as Alex shifted his bulk. He said, "Mah puir bones say we must've started on th' meetin' part ay the business."

"Your bones would be correct," Sten said. "When we get some light on the subject, you'll find a few bodies crammed in here with us. Two of them have crushed larynxes. That was you. The other has what looks like a second mouth. In her neck. That was my bad. When I cut the power cable, I also managed to cut someone's throat before I blacked out. My back is sticky, so I assume I'm lying in the scrote's blood."

Silence. Sten hoped his heavy-worlder friend was coming out of his drug-induced state and was starting to get a handle on things.

"What do we do next, wee Sten?" he finally asked. "Ah huvnae th' faintest Scooby."

Before Sten could answer three things happened:

A red pinlight blinked into life just above his head.

His com unit crackled and buzzed in his ears.

Ida started talking as only Ida could, by blistering his ears with a stream of what Sten could only think were Rom curses.

Then the world settled a little more about Sten's shoulders, and he could make out what she was saying.

"Drakh and fall back in it," she growled. "I've been trying to roust you scrotes out of that little cubby hole you're hiding in for two small forever's."

"Well, now you've found us," Sten said. "The only problem is we don't know where the clot we are. Our minds seem to be stuffed with mud."

Ida grunted. "Something much worse and smellier is more likely," she said. "Actually, from my readings they hit you with a couple of hypoguns. Nothing life threatening. But you might be missing some of your short term memory for awhile."

She fell silent for a moment. Sten could imagine her aboard the *Storm*, punching in numbers. Weighing the telemeter stream she was getting from his and Alex's implanted Med chips.

Mental course correction as things became clearer still: Ida wouldn't be aboard the *Storm*, which was still in the yard. She'd be aboard the new ship Mahoney had wrangled for them. The *Jo'l Cash*.

"So where the clot are we?" Sten asked.

Ida said, "You're in a tool shed about three levels below the bar where you started out."

"But what about the mutineers?" Sten asked. "The guys Snilch told us about."

"Snilch?" Alex broke in. "Who the clot is Snilch?"

Ida ignored him. She said: "Hello! Anybody home. Oh, for drakh's sake, don't you get it, Sten? We've been conned. Snookered. Flimflammed. Snilch was lying through that little twisted beak of his."

Silence as Sten took this in and Alex tried to come up to speed. A little more memory filtered in, and he suddenly had that awful feeling one gets when things have gone very wrong indeed.

And there was only one direction the Finger of Blame could be pointed.

"Drakh and fall back in it is right," he groaned.

Then he another gut-wrenching thought: "Those beings we killed? By any chance were they…"

"Himmenops," Ida finished for him. "A squad of Venatora's superwomen."

"How in hell—"

"Never mind the how," Ida said. "It'll come to you by and by. Meanwhile, I'm sure you'll recall that those Himmenops have many largish sisters with pissy moods at the best of times. And right now they are on the way looking for paybacks."

For a crazy, heat-filled moment Sten thought of asking if Venatora was with them. Instead he said, "Then you'd better hurry and get us the clot out of here."

"Roger, that," Ida said. Sten imagined her fingers flying across her beloved boards as she made the patch.

Then, in the voice of a Gypsy witch, she intoned: "Let there be light."

And just like that the darkness vanished to be replaced by glaring yellow lights beaming from the ceiling.

"Ooch," Alex said, rubbing his eyes. "Th' lass has nae gentleness in her. She jist hits ye an' goes about her merry way."

Sten found himself in a hidey-hole that he only vaguely recalled. There was no doubt that it was a toolroom—it was crowded with benches and machines and various mechanical devices, all glistening with oil and heavy grease.

The room was small—there was barely space for Sten and his heavy-worlder companion, whose bulk filled one whole side— much less the ghastly remains of two very dead Himmenops. Even in death their musculature was such that Sten found it hard to imagine anyone could have bested them in a hand-to-hand fight. But the odd tilt of their necks and the deep impressions in their necks made by Kilgour's steely grip told the tale.

Next to Sten was another Himmenops, her nearly naked body twisted in her last desperate efforts to breathe. A bloody second mouth gaped below her chiseled chin. Sten remembered carving that second mouth just before he felt the sting in his arm from a hypno gun.

Then everything went blank.

With difficulty, he climbed to his knees and reached for the airlock's wheel. It refused to turn. Sten shrugged, flexed his wrist just so, and his knife leaped from its fleshy sheath in his arm and his fingers curled around its slender haft.

Anticipating his actions, Ida said, "Unless you're suited up, better drop the idea of cutting yourself out of your little home away from home. When the others fled, they dumped the atmosphere."

Alex spoke up. "Cheers for the warnin', darlin'."

"Don't call me darling," Ida snapped.

"Oh, aye," Alex said. "Ah was thinkin' on anither word, but thought it micht be impolite."

He was sitting up now, pushing one body onto the other to give himself more room. He rolled his shoulders and cracked his knuckles.

"Ah'm Red Rory of th' toolroom," he intoned.

"Who the clottin' clot is Red Rory?" Ida demanded.

Sten jumped in. "Shut up, Ida," he pleaded. "Or he'll tell you. In infinite detail. Now, about your plans to get us the clot out of here?"

Ida said, "I've tracked the atmospheric supply network and will have that fixed in a jiff and a half. Plus I've got three of our Marines on the way."

Kilgour frowned. "Marines? We have Marines?" Then light dawned. "Oh, aye. We hae a full crew ay squadies noo, don't we?" he said. "They'll be makin' ye a bonny admiral affair ye ken it, wee Sten."

Sten couldn't help but grin. He'd felt a little otherwordly when command of the sleek Radoslaw class fighter had been turned over to him. The *Jo'l Cash* had a crew of 75, missile batteries, chain-guns—all the things a young being would pine for when heading into combat.

Of course, he didn't have the faintest idea how to run a ship of that size and sophistication, so Mahoney had thoughtfully provided them with a real ship's captain, complete with graying hair, steely eyes, and an attitude that plainly showed she did not appreciate taking orders from a mere lieutenant who was about the age of her twenty-something son.

The captain was also incompetent as clot. It was the captain, after all, who had gotten them into this mess.

In Sten's experience incompetent people, stupid people, knew their flaws and resented the clot out of anyone with even a gram of ability, and took it out on them every chance they could.

Ida's voice broke through. "You still with us, Sten?"

"For better or worse," Sten said.

"Well, you'd better come up with something better than that," Ida said, "or this whole exercise will be a complete waste."

"Cheers fur remindin' us, mah wee tub of Rom," Alex said.

He patted the cheek of one of the corpses. "An' here we waur thinkin' evr'thin' was hunky dory."

CHAPTER THIRTEEN

THE GOD BOX

Sten didn't know what "hunky dory" meant and had no intention of asking Alex. The last time he'd stepped into that mess, it had gotten him the "Spotted Snake" story, which had taken two small eternities to tell. And then delivered a payoff that left him feeling like he'd just completed—barely—a Mantis Section survival test through the parasitic swamps of Clamitus III.

But if it meant things were a mound of drakh waiting to be stepped in, then that exactly described the mission from the moment he, Alex, Ida and Doc had boarded the *Jo'l Cash*.

It also underscored the dilemma he found himself in now, trapped in a toolroom with Alex, surrounded by the corpses of Venatora's women.

Originally, the plan had been to be as low key as possible. When the ship took on supplies, they'd blend in with the dock workers and crew and quietly make contact with the captain, who would stash them in a spare berth until the vessel was well on its way.

Only then would their presence be explained. It was a carefully crafted explanation that had been pored over by Rykor's best psyops team.

To begin with, the very word "mutiny" had nasty connotations and was to be avoided at all costs. Even the most benign officer must look at her crew at times and wonder if they'd all secretly like to jam her in a tube and deep space her.

If badly handled, the news that a real crew had rebelled against their officers would spread through the ship at warp speed and soon everyone aboard would be unnerved, staring suspiciously at one another and concocting all sorts of conspiracy theories. Eventually, it would spread to other ships and then on to rage across the fleets, like one of those ancient plagues that demoralized, then destroyed entire navies.

Morale, Sten thought, would be so far under the drakh house it might never surface again.

Then, as Mahoney had carefully explained, there was the even bigger picture of what was at stake:

The Emperor's prestige.

The loyalty of his supporters and allies.

The carnivorous gleam in his enemies' eyes as they saw him stripped and robbed by small-time thugs like a bumbling spaceport tourist who had wandered down the wrong alley.

They also didn't want to announce themselves to the mutineers aboard the *Flame* until the last possible moment. The idea was to suddenly pop up just a little outside of what the mutineers would consider their safe zone, and then very slowly, very laboriously, begin negotiations.

"Boredom works wonders in times like these," Mahoney said. "They're all on a hair trigger and so when you slow things down it'll drive them half mad. Then, when you do make the offer, they'll be so glad to see the back of it they'll agree to all sorts of nonsense."

Meanwhile, Mahoney said, he wanted Sten to test the limits of that agreed upon "safe zone," probing here and there for signs of weakness.

"The sooner we can catch them out before the deal is official, the easier and neater this whole thing will be," Mahoney had said.

And, stretching over all the whole clotting thing, was the need to keep the Empire at large from ever learning what had happened in the pirate-ridden Possnet Sector.

"All business must be conducted in absolute secrecy," Mahoney said. "And I can't stress the word strongly enough."

Unfortunately, it was a word that had apparently gone missing from Captain W'lson's vocabulary.

At first, everything seemed to be going fine. Sten and the others blended in with the workers, overseeing the loading of a large container marked "Engine Room Supplies." In reality, it contained various highly classified weapons, tools, gear, and devices produced in Mantis Section laboratories and was known by everyone in the trade as a "God Box."

Or, as Alex put it: "If yoo're up drakh creek missin' a paddle, a God Box works faster'n prayer."

Just as they got it stowed in an out-of-the-way spot in the hold, a young Marine approached them.

"Which one of you is Captain Sten?" he asked.

Still a little dazed from the toolroom misadventure, Sten hesitated a beat. Oh, that's right. He was—temporarily—a captain, not a lieutenant. A bizarre thought intruded: maybe his pay check would reflect the promotion. Then, quickly realizing how mentally off course he was, he thought: Sure, Sten. Sure. In the reality that is *Imperial Personnel: Payment of...* A bottle-eyed clerk would probably dock him for some nonsense like "being out of grade."

Pulling himself back to the moment, Sten said, "That would be me, corporal. Do you have a berth for us?"

The corporal saluted, then said. "Not exactly, sir. The Skipper wants to speak to you first."

He motioned for them to follow, and with some trepidation, Sten and the others fell in behind him.

To Sten's dismay, instead of leading them to a quiet retreat away from the hubbub of a working Ship of the Line, the Marine took them through the main passageways, where they drew the immediate attention—and curious stares—of the crewmembers. Then a double bay door opened before them, and Sten realized they were stepping into the bridge, where—to his horror—the captain had arranged for them to receive the full honors due an important admiral's chief aide, who also happened to be his nephew.

As pipes shrilled throughout the *Jo'l Cash*, the drawn up Marine squad snapped to attention with much slamming of boots, Sten half jumped across the intervening space and grabbed the captain by her epaulettes.

"Stop this," he hissed. "At once."

Captain W'lson stared at him in total disbelief, going from deathly pale to purple rage in milliseconds.

She started to protest, but Sten tightened his grip. "Get them out of here," he said, indicating the Marines.

Then he waved at all the officers gathered for the ceremony. "Get them all out of here."

W'lson sputtered something incomprehensible, but before she could continue, Sten said, "If you don't do as I say immediately,

I'll get Mahoney on the horn and you'll be lucky if your next posting is on an ice planet."

Her dignity in tatters, W'lson seemed unable to move. Sten wondered how the clot she would react if the ship were under fire.

Fortunately, her XO stepped into the breach. A slender, well built human with a hawk face and a healthy cynical nature that had allowed him to survive under the incompetent rule of his captain, Lieutenant Mk'wolf quickly sussed out the situation and got everything under control.

He moved among the other officers. There were nods and whispers. Shared understanding that once again their commander had them all balancing on the edge of a career-ending precipice. Whispered orders. A shuffle of feet. And in a few minutes the bridge was cleared.

When they were gone, W'lson shook Sten off and drew herself up. "This is an outrage," she said. "An unforgivable violation of every tradition of our service."

Sten said, "Did you or did you not receive explicit orders to preserve the secrecy of this mission?"

"Of course I did," she replied. "But I interpreted that to mean that those orders applied to outsiders. Not the crew of my own ship."

Anger nearly overwhelmed Sten. "You *interpreted*? Why, you silly puffed up piece of—"

But the Captain wasn't having any. Her own temper boiled over.

"Just look at you," she said, making a wide gesture that took in the four strange beings standing in front of her. "You're not even in uniform."

At any other time, Sten's odd sense of humor would've cut in. Because they were indeed a motley crew.

Sten wore greasy overalls, with a tear in one sleeve that ran from the elbow to the cuff, thanks to a quick draw practice session with his knife.

Alex, the tubby heavy-worlder, had let his beard grow for the mission and had the look of a red-bearded barbarian about to attack a Roman garrison at Hadrian's Wall.

Ida was unabashedly Gypsy, sporting rings on every finger, huge earrings on her lobes, sparkling necklaces cascading down her chins. All topped off with a billowy shift of many colors tucked into super plus-size overalls.

And then there was Doc, the team's psy-warfare op, who looked like nothing more than a meter-high super-cuddly teddy bear, instead of a *Blyrchynaus*, one of the deadliest and most cunning species in the empire.

And it was Doc who at that moment had the wisdom to intervene. He sidled up to the Captain, and from the prickling sensation running up and down Sten's spine, he knew that Doc had turned on his psionic talents full force.

"You must pardon young Sten, Captain," he said, practically purring. "He's been under a great deal of stress of late."

Although he'd witnessed the effect Doc had on beings before, he was still astonished when he saw W'lson visibly relax, a smile wreathing her broad face.

She reached down as if to pat Doc, who gently steered her hand away. Sten could tell it was all Doc could do to keep from biting it.

"Why, yes, I can understand that," W'lson said. Then she looked over at Sten. "Perhaps you would all like a nice cup of tea," she said. "I usually put on a pot this time of day."

"Tea! What an excellent idea," Doc said. Then he took W'lson by the hand. "Why don't we adjourn to the comfort of your quarters, Captain?" he suggested. "Where we can all get to know one another a little better."

W'lson started babbling. "Yes, yes… Get to know one another. What an excellent idea. We'll go to my cabin. Have a little tea. Maybe a nice hot scone to accompany it…"

And with W'lson mumbling happily, Doc nodded at Sten and the others to follow, and in a few minutes they were all safely out of sight—if not out of mind—of the ship's officers and crew.

CHAPTER FOURTEEN

VENATORA

Unfortunately, the damage was done, and before long word of the strange doings aboard the *Jo'l Cash* reached the lovely ears of Venatora.

After spreading several fistfuls of bribe money about, she obtained a very good description of the young lieutenant whose arrival had caused such a stir aboard the Imperial ship.

"I knew he was the law," she told Marta, her El Segundo. "And he's clearly hiding something."

Although Marta was as big and muscular as the other Zabanya guardswomen, her features were more delicate—her face heart-shaped, with a beauty mark at the left-hand corner of her lip.

She considered Venatora's remarks, then asked, "Unless I'm missing something, Ma'am, that doesn't necessarily mean it has anything to do with our business, does it?"

"I'm probably being paranoid," Venatora said. "But if it weren't for paranoia, one of my royal sisters would have killed and eaten me long ago."

"I'll try to find out more, Ma'am," Marta said. "But it's difficult. The Imperial sector of the port is under the tightest security our spies have ever seen."

"Even more reason to suspect that Sten is the Emperor's man," Venatora said. "When spies are poking about, you know something is going on."

The pirate queen reflected a few moments. Then a smile of pleasure lit her ebony features.

"All that Imperium X," she murmured. "I've dreamed of a chance like this since the night Melipona crept into my room with murder on her mind and a dagger in her fist." She chuckled. "She didn't know I'd been tipped off and was waiting behind the door.

Pillows stuffed under the blankets. Such a simple, even childish, trick."

Marta laughed. "There was nothing childish about the knife you used on her, Ma'am," she said.

"No, not at all," Venatora said.

She drew a long, bejeweled blade whose sheath dangled from the slender golden chain encircling her narrow waist. She turned it this way and that, admiring how light rippled along its surface.

"The last of your rivals, Ma'am," Marta murmured, reflecting on that long ago memory.

"Oh, there will be others," Venatora said. "The hive is already reaching its limit. We need to expand—and expand quickly—or I'll have a whole army of envious princesses at my throat, all vying to rule my Himmenops sisters."

Marta nodded. "And to fight them you'll need money, won't you, Ma'am?" she said.

Venatora laughed. "We'll need wads of the stuff," she said. "More money than we made during my whole career chasing the crumbs the Eternal Emperor leaves scattered about."

"We'll have an entire space-train of crumbs, won't we, Ma'am" Marta said, enjoying the little joke. "Exactly one hundred and twenty-five kilometers' worth of Imperium X for your treasury."

Her lips twitched, and Venatora found the movement of the beauty mark enchanting.

"Indeed we will," Venatora said. "But we don't want to fall into the trap of underestimating the Emperor. He'll have a plan to deal with those mutineers."

Venatora flipped the blade end over end, snatching it from the air with a flourish.

"Mutineers!" She shook her head in mock dismay. "Oh, how that must gall him. Traitors in his own service. He'll want their heads."

"But the mutineers are demanding amnesty, Ma'am," Marta said. "If he wants his Imperium X back, he'll have to let them live."

"That's our hole card," Venatora said. "We must make the mutineers believe that the Emperor won't keep any promises he makes. That he'll kill them the first chance he gets. Of course, to convince them otherwise, he'll have to send his very best man."

"And you think this Lieutenant Sten might be that man?" Marta asked, looking doubtful. "He's so young."

Venatora gave a low, throaty chuckle. "Deliciously so," she said. "However…there was something about him. Something…" And she let the rest trail off.

Marta sniffed.

She's jealous, Venatora thought. How charming. She knew if she just touched Marta, the woman would melt. Such was her power over her warrior women.

And then she wondered if she would have the same effect on Sten. Her heart fluttered. If she was honest with herself, she'd have to admit he had a definite effect on her.

She shook herself. Enough of that.

"Very well," she said, all business once again. "If we can't get past Imperial security in the little time we have remaining, then we'll have to get them to come to us."

"What do you have in mind, Ma'am?" Marta asked.

"A black marble," Venatora replied. "We just need to find the best place to drop it…then see where it rolls out."

CHAPTER FIFTEEN

PORT CHINEN

Of all the wild outposts on the Empire's frontier, Port Chinen was hands, tentacles, and even claws-down the wildest.

As Alex put it, "It's like some wee joker turned th' Empire on its side an' aw th' bampots fell out an' landed here."

Set upon a barren planet with only rudimentary life forms, the port sat at crossroads that, until only recently, led nowhere.

With the discovery in the region of a veritable mother lode of Imperium X, Chinen exploded like the mining boom towns of old. It mushroomed out from what had once been a small, unimportant Imperial space fortress set between two rugged peaks into a chaotic warren of ramshackle buildings and facilities run by the mining companies and independent operators—all crowding around the Imperial space fortress right up to the fortress gates.

And so when Sten and Alex guided their grav car past the last security checkpoint—leaving the relative peace and order of the base—they descended into sheer pandemonium.

Massive vehicles lumbered about—using sheer size to impose their will on anything or anyone smaller. It was as if all laws of traffic and common sense had been abandoned in favor of commerce by suicidal nerve. Hundreds of beings unfortunate enough, or brave enough, to be on foot took their lives in their hands as they dodged in and out of this deadly melee.

Alex had barely poked the nose of their grav car past the gate when they were nearly run down by a hundred-kiloton tanker.

Their com units shrieked unintelligible warnings while the tanker's enormous robotic arms reached out to literally push them aside—right into the path of a gigantic container sledge.

"Look out!" Sten shouted as Kilgour jerked the stick to the side just in time.

He shook his fist at the sledge, shouting, "Hamshanker idjiots!"

Which led them directly into the path of yet another mechanical behemoth. Kilgour narrowly avoided being T-boned and accelerated onward.

Before they could be tangled in another deadly encounter, Sten reached over, pushed Kilgour's hand aside, and punched on the automatic override.

Immediately, things calmed down—relatively speaking. Every few seconds brought on another near disaster, but now all the various onboard computers running the vehicles synced with one another and they were soon speeding in and out of traffic with relative ease. Especially now that no sentient beings such as stubborn Scotsmen were involved in guiding the vehicles. They'd let the onboard computer use is cameras, radar, sonar and countless other devices specifically designed for this sort of chaos.

"If we're gonna clottin' die," Sten said, "let's do it in a sensible shootout with the bad guys. I prefer that to being turned into road grease."

"We're lettin' bots and computers run our bloody lives," Alex complained. "Besides—ah like to drive."

"Well, speaking as your beloved first lieutenant," Sten said, "I'd advise you to stifle that impulse and take up something sane, like bull leaping."

"Why would a body want tae jump ower a puir bull?" Kilgour asked.

"It's just a guess," Sten said, "but I suppose it's to avoid the horns."

Kilgour muttered something unintelligible—whether a curse or a compliment, his accent was so thick Sten couldn't always tell.

Then he said, "Aren't ye e'en a wee bit leery abit this smuggler bloke we're supposed tae meet?"

"Sure I am," Sten said. "But we can't pass up the chance that the info is golden."

Kilgour snorted. "Ah'm guessin' Mahoney said that."

"He did," Sten said.

Alex, sighed, "Ah, weel, that sounds like the wee general," he said. "Ah suppose there's nothin' fur us tae do but stick uir heads into th' lion's gob and see if he's hungry."

In a largish nutshell, this is exactly how Sten felt about the upcoming meeting.

Not long after the W'lson debacle, Mk'wolf had escorted a strange little creature into their quarters. His eyes were little black beads that were constantly on the move on either side of a twisted, beak-like nose. His bald head was ludicrously small and pink as a human baby's buttocks.

He had a manner so nervous that his principle tentacles were in constant motion. Flick, flick. Polishing his bald head. Flick, flick. Cleaning out one of the two little orbs on either side of his head that Sten assumed were ears. Flick, flick. And then the tip of a tentacle was reaching for what Sten presumed was a nostril.

Sten gave the XO a tired look. He said, "This the guy the captain was talking about?"

"In the flesh, or whatever he calls that saggy stuff hanging off his bones," Mk'wolf replied. "My first thought was to get rid of him as soon as the captain turned her back," he said. "But then he said something that I thought might be worth your attention."

"And that something was…"

"A name," Mk'wolf said. He turned to the little being.

"Tell him, Snilch," he said. "Tell him the name."

Snilch spoke up in a high squeaky voice. "The name's Gregor. That's what I heard. Bigger'n life. Gregor!"

Sten said, "What makes you think that name is important to us? And by the way, who the clot do you think we are?"

"Who you are…" Snilch said. Flick, flick. "Why, it ain't for me to say who you are." Flick, flick. "You know who you are, matey. And ya' likes the name Gregor. I can tell. Can't hide drakh from old Snilch. Ask anybody on Chinen." Flick, flick. "Anybody at all."

He heard Doc mutter something like "classic," and assumed the bloodthirsty Blyrchynaus was scratching about for the proper nut box to put Snilch in.

Sten looked at Mk'wolf for help.

"It's like this, lieutenant," Mk'wolf said. "Snilch here was babbling on like crazy…just like he's doing now…and just as we were ready to space him he says this name, 'Gregor'.

"Now everybody knows that Captain Gregor came through Chinen with a whole space-train of Imperium X. As a matter of fact, he took on some supplies here. I think it was their last stop."

Sten nodded. He knew this to be true. He had seen the Port's master log.

"Anyway, sir," Mk'wolf went on, "Captain Gregor's long gone." He jabbed a thumb at Snilch. "Then suddenly this little bit of filth is talking about needing supplies for Captain Gregor...and the *Flame*."

Sten turned to Snilch. "Tell me," he said.

Snilch tiny eyes swept Sten's face, then back again. Tentacles going. Flick, flick. The head. Ear. The beak. Flick, flick. Sten imagined it was the longest the little thief had gone without talking in whatever lifespan his DNA had decreed.

Finally, he said, "It's like this, Cheena old matey." Flick, flick. "I have, what you call...yeah, a reputation, Cheena. A reputation. My information is always sweet. And true."

Put a tentacle to his thin lips and kissed it.

"Sweet," he said.

"How much?" Sten said.

Snilch raised a tentacle. "Wait up, Cheena. What's the hurry? Say...if you're in such a hurry, maybe we ought to take that into..." Flick, flick... "what'ca call...consideration." Flick, flick. "Yeah, matey. Let's consider the consideration." Flick, flick.

Sten said, "Here's what you need to understand—*matey*! You may have useful information for us. On the other hand, you may not. So there is no worth we can put on it in advance. Tell me. And then we'll decide its value."

"That's not how old Snilch does business, Cheena," Snilch said. "Not how I do business at all. Ask anybody. They'll tell you. I gets me price or I gets to me feet."

With that he rose from his chair. Then squeaked as Alex put a massive hand on his bald pate and pushed him down so hard the bottom of the chair bowed.

Ida said, "You know, boys, it just came to me that this could be a very profitable situation. I can make our baksheesh budget as big or small as I please."

"Nobody can fiddle th' books bettern'you, my bonny gypsy lass," Alex said.

"But, where is the profit?" Doc wanted to know.

She pointed at Snilch. "He talks for free. But in the report I say we paid him a couple of hundred grand." She grinned at Snilch. "I'm sure you'd be happy to sign a receipt, won't you honey?"

Snilch gobbled. "Free? Snilch does not do free." Flick, flick. "He would not do free for his mother, curse her soul, she was an old bitch anyway." Flick, flick. "No, no. Free is not happening. You pay…two hundred thousand is too little, I think…you pay…I talk. Everybody happy."

Ida looked at Mk'wolf. "We'll split it five ways," she said, as if not hearing a word of Snipe's counter. "So you'll get your fair share. After all, you've made all this possible."

The XO grinned. "That's very generous of you, ma'am."

Eyes aglow, Ida patted his handsome face. "It's my nature," she said. "Generosity is my middle name."

Doc motioned to Alex. "Fetch my tools, would you sergeant?"

Alex opened an overhead bin and took out a large black box. He set it beside Doc, who beamed with pleasure.

"Oh, my toys," he said. "My wonderful, wonderful toys. It's been so long since I've been able to play with them."

He opened the box, revealing gleaming instruments, all sharp and pointed and nasty looking. There were trays of vials and catheters and tubing. Compartments with bone saws and pincers.

"Hello, boys," he said fondly, stroking the instruments. He looked up at the others. "They're old fashioned," he said, "but you know me. I prefer the old tried and true methods of eliciting information."

"In some circles it's called torture," Ida told Mk'wolf, who nodded with interest. "And legally it's forbidden to torture a prisoner. But, you know, there are laws and there are laws."

"I'm just guessing," Mk'wolf said, "but I'll bet those laws don't apply to people like you."

"Exactly," Ida said. "They don't apply to people like us. There are some very artful loopholes."

"Who are you guys?" Snilch shrieked. "Torture? What's this torture? You can't torture—"

He swallowed whatever he was going to say next when Doc lifted the bone saw off its hook. He smiled at Snilch whose tentacles were going, flick, flick.

"I know that tentacles are mostly cartilage," Doc said. "But the muscle can be rather thick and stringy."

He raised up the saw, light dancing on its serrated steel surface. "However, this little darling should do the trick admirably."

Snilch talked.

CHAPTER SIXTEEN

THE BLACK MARBLE

By smell alone the Reek's Rest more than lived up to its name.

The overpowering stench had Sten and Alex retching half a klick before they even reached the bar, which sported a battered sign with a picture of a snarling black reek with a white streak down its back.

And when they walked in, the smell was so overpowering they were almost knocked out of their boots. It was as if someone had done a bad of job of burying a reek the size of a mastodon, whose corpse gave off every imaginable odor as its caustic fluids and secretions rotted slowly away.

Unfortunately, since they were posing as old port hands accustomed to the foulest of odors, they had to act like Reek's Rest was a veritable homebar away from homebar.

They fired up a couple of t'bacs, sucking deeply on the nicotine to settle their suddenly nervous bellies as they strode ever so casually to the bar where a blond behemoth of a woman held forth.

She looked them over as they approached, pasting a well-practiced lascivious smile on her big pink face.

In a booming voice she intoned: "Big Byrtha's the name, and boozin's my game, so belly up to the bar, boys, belly up."

The crowded room was so dimly lit that Sten doubted anyone had noticed the exchange, much less heard it over the bar sounds. Even so, he kept watch, letting Alex handle the big woman.

Kilgour turned on the charm. Laughing, he said, "I love those auld vids too, my bonnie. Next, yoo'll be sayin, 'What's yer pleasure, wee jimmies?' An, 'Are those pistols in yer pockets, lads, ur are yer jist glad tae see me?'"

Big Byrtha guffawed. Looking Alex up and down, and clearly liking what she saw, she said, "From yer manner of talk, if yer don't mind me sayin', yer must be a kilt wearin' man."

"Guilty as twice boiled haggis yer are, lass," he said. He whacked his big chest. "Ah'm Scots through and through."

"So, where's yer kilt, big man?" Big Byrtha asked.

"It shrunk in th' wash," Kilgour said. "Ah was in danger ay showin' off me nethers."

Big Byrtha liked that, too. Laughing heartily, she slammed a meaty fist on the bar. Then she grabbed a bottle and poured two shots.

"From the cut a yer jibs," she said, "I'm figger'n yer both Stregg men," she said.

"That we be," Kilgour said, throwing back a shot.

Sten followed suit, and Big Byrtha poured two more. "From the looks of yer," she said, "If I were in the guessin' business, yer new to Chinen."

"An' yoo'd be guessin' correctly, mah braw beauty," Alex said.

"Then, here's another guess," Big Byrtha continued. "Yer have the look of working stiffs, but the manner of businessmen. If my guess is on the money, which are yer?"

Alex waggled a hand back and forth. "A wee ay baith, lass," he said. "Jist like our visit tae yer braw establishment. We're haur fur a bit ay pleasure, but hopin' fur a bit ay business. If thaur is any tae be had."

She grinned, saying, "Were yer mebbe thinkin' Big Byrtha might be of help in yer business?"

"Indeed we were," Alex said.

Big Byrtha glanced around the bar, as if assuring privacy, then motioned for Alex to come closer.

"Then have a whisper in my shell like, Mr. Kilt Man," she said.

Kilgour leaned in until his head was nearly touching Big Byrtha's. "We bin chin waggin' with this wee scrote name ay Snilch," he said. "He tauld us yer might be able tae help wi' a wee problem that's bin devilin' us."

At the mention of the name, Big Byrtha frowned and drew away. Started polishing the bar with a dirty rag.

"Snilch," she said, in tones that made the name sound lower than reek droppings. "I never have doings with that little snitch. Just lookin' at him makes me bum break out in boils."

"Now, now, lass," Kilgour soothed. "We sussed 'at he was a

bad a body right off. But it was information we were after. The vital sort." Alex sighed a regretful sigh. "An' when yoo're efter information, yer cannae always be too choosy ay yer company," he said.

Big Byrtha sniffed. "And I'm supposin' Snilch said I might be in possession of the sort of information yer after," she said.

Sten noted her tone was easier now. The Kilgour charm was doing its job.

"'At he did," Alex said.

"So what sort of information are yer after, Mr. Kilt Man?" she asked.

"Th' kind 'at makes a handsome profit fur baith ay us," Alex said. He tapped his chest. "Money fur th' likes ay us." And he gave Big Byrtha his most winning smile. "An' a bundle a credits fur yer as well, mah wee lass."

At this, Big Byrtha plunked down another shot glass and poured herself a Stregg, then two more for Alex and Sten.

She downed her drink then put a hand on one ample hip.

"I'm all ears," she said. Then, laughing, she added, "And all boobs and hips and belly and butt, boys." As she spoke, she ran her hands down her body, demonstrating.

Alex gave each part an admiring look, shook his head in awe, then proceeded to spin the tale he and Sten had worked out.

Mostly they told the truth—well, the truth according to Snilch. It seems that a certain Captain Gregor of the *Flame* was well known in black market circles for selling ship's stores and supplies. He used falsified bills of lading, broken containers, spoiled food, faulty equipment and any semi-reasonable excuse he could phony up to skirt regulations. A few times, it was said, he'd even sold certain weapons on the black market—a firing squad offense if there ever was one.

Snilch claimed it was also well known that Big Byrtha served as a middlewoman in many lucrative black market transactions and was reputed to be a "square shooter" when it came to underworld business.

"So yer think I've got somethin' goin' on with Gregor now, do yer?" Big Byrtha asked.

Sten thought it interesting that she didn't out and out deny any of Snilch's claims.

"So Snilch said, lass," Alex replied. "Mind ye, he didnae speak easily. Even after crossin' his palms wi' silver, we had te thump him a bit aboot th' head an' shoulders."

Big Byrtha laughed. "Wish I'd been there to glimmer it," she said. "I have a notion to wring his neck meself every now and then."

She gave Alex a smoldering look. "You're not thinkin' of smackin' poor little Byrtha about, are yer my darlin' Mr. Kilt Man?"

Alex looked aghast. "Never!" he proclaimed. Then he grinned. "Weel, mebbe a bit if a wee kinky mince is tae yer likin'.'"

"Wait'll I see what's under the kilt, sweetie," Byrtha replied with a low laugh.

Kilgour gave her a wink and said. "Ah can only hiner an' pray, lass. Only hiner and pray." Then he grew serious. "So, lass, it comes tae this. Snilch says there is a Gregor deal afoot an' yoo're handlin' it. But this isn't an ordinary Gregor deal. This time we're talkin' about a coople ay hundred kilos ay Imperium X. Swatched right off th' *Flame*, Snilch says. If thae's the case, a bonnie profit could be made for th' three of us."

Big Byrtha just stared at him.

"Do ya' ken what Ah'm gettin' at lass?" Alex prodded.

"Yer want to hijack Gregor's goods," Big Byrtha said. "And yer want me to help yer. Fer a price, that is."

"Exactly, lass," Kilgour said. "Smart as new paint, ye are, lass. Smart as new paint."

Big Byrtha motioned to one of her assistants to take over her post. She nodded toward a door next to the bar.

"Let's go into my office and talk business, Mr. Kilt Man," she said.

As they followed her big, waggling behind into the office, Sten had a sudden vision of a fish swallowing a baited hook.

And the fish wore Sten's face.

CHAPTER SEVENTEEN

OUTNUMBERED AND OUTGUNNED

Kilgour looked gloomily around their toolroom prison, gingerly shifting his bulk away from the nearest corpse.

"If ye thought it was a trap, lad," he said, "Why did'ne ye warn yer auld comrade in arms an' other low pursuits?"

Sten shrugged. "Guess I just got caught up in the wonderfulness of your con job."

"As it turns out," Alex said, "it was nae me who was doin' the connin'."

He snorted, disgusted with himself. "'Mister Kilt Man,' she called me. Whit can Ah say—it went tae me noggin, it did."

"It was a lower extremity than your head she was aiming for," Sten said. "Much lower."

Then full realization sunk in. Sten groaned. So much for all that Mantis training.

"Mahoney's going to kill us," he said. "Then he'll tan our bodies and hang us out for bayonet practice."

But as he spoke, one of Alex's corpses started making very undeadlike sounds—choking and gasping and flopping about.

"Sten, me wee lad," Alex exclaimed, "ah think thes wee lass has returned frae th' deid!

"For God's sake, help her," Sten said. Thinking hope against hope that maybe something could be salvaged from this mess after all.

With both hands, Alex started pumping the big woman's chest. Then pinched her mouth open and blew in a mighty breath.

More choking. More flopping. Sten looked closer at the woman's face. Despite the agony-contorted features, he thought he recognized her as one of the Zabanya guardswomen who had accompanied Venatora at the Xypaca match.

She had a little beauty mark on the left hand corner of her bottom lip. Yes. The very same woman. He recalled wondering if she might be Venatora's second in command. If so…

"Keep it up," Sten said.

He clicked his com unit. "Ida! Are you there, Ida?"

The Rom woman's sarcastic voice came crackling back. "Of course, I'm here, you big clot," she said. "And quit yelling. Last thing I need is another eardrum transplant."

"What's the ETA on the jarheads?" Sten demanded.

"If by jarheads, you mean our lovely marines," Ida replied, "they'll be there in two shakes. I've slaved the atmosphere unit to my station, so you should have breathable air any second now..." A moment later: "Okay, you're good to go. Now say 'thank you, oh wise and beauteous Ida.'"

"Knock it off," Sten said. "One of these dead women has decided she's the sister to Mister Lazarus.

"Lazarus!" Ida said. "What in the flaming drakh pit are you talking about, Sten?"

Sten said, "I mean that she's not so dead after all. But to keep it that way, we're going to need a medpak. Fast!"

"Ah, trading stock," Ida said. The idea warming her Rom heart. A brief silence.

Then, "Okay, the marines are here. And they've got a medpak. Now, go get 'em, boys."

Sten flexed the fingers of his right hand and the knife sphinctered out into his palm. Quickly, he carved a man-sized square into the toolroom's wall. Then leaned back and kicked.

There was screech of metal straining against metal. He kicked again, and the area he'd cut ripped away, clanging to the floor outside. Air flooded in with a whoosh and Sten felt his ears pop.

Lt. Mk'wolf's hawk-like face appeared in the opening. His brow was wrinkled with worry, but when he saw that Sten was apparently unhurt, the frown turned into a grin.

He offered a helping hand. "Better get a move on, sir," he said. "They aren't too far behind us."

Sten grabbed and heaved himself out. He pointed at Alex, who was bent over the thrashing figure of the woman.

"Get a medic working on her," he told Mk'wolf. "I don't care what kind of hypejuice you pump into her, just so long as she can stand on her own two feet for a couple of minutes."

"Gotcha, boss," Mk'wolf said and motioned for one of the young marines to come forward.

Seconds later the Marine medic had taken over from Alex. He slapped a breather over her face, holding it in place with one hand, while he sorted through his medpak with the other.

Keeping her down with the weight of his body, he shot her full of wakeup juice, recharged the hypogun and did it again.

She jumped like she'd been hit with an electrical charge. She sat straight up, carrying the medic with her. Sten motioned for another marine to join him.

"Help him restrain her," he said. "Then haul her out and get her undercover."

He heard Alex shout a warning and an AM2 round sizzled past his face. It hit the toolroom wall, molten metal splattering.

Then more rounds were coming in and while Kilgour and Mk'wolf laid down bursts of answering fire, Sten and another marine helped the medic drag the wounded woman out of the toolroom.

At first she made no resistance, but as they pushed her behind the barrier of shipping containers Alex had muscled into place she started struggling and making horrible gargling noises through her injured throat.

"Here, now," Alex said, reaching for the woman. "Yer gonna get yerself kilt!"

He grabbed her by the scruff of the neck and hauled her to safety just as another burst of AM2 rounds buzzed around them like angry hornets.

"Return fire," Sten shouted. "But for clot's sake, don't shoot anybody. Just keep their heads down."

Easier said than done. The enemy fire was so hot and heavy Sten and others could barely move without exposing themselves.

On their right, Sten spotted a squad of Himmenops leapfrogging from cover to cover, while their sisters kept up the withering assault.

Any minute now and they'd have Sten's team flanked and at their mercy. After that, well, somehow, he doubted they had a word for mercy in the Himmenops native language.

Sten looked desperately about, then spotted an enormous yellow crane parked in one corner. This was the obvious place for Venatora's women to take cover and prepare for the final assault.

He noted the crane's three-story-high hoisting boom hanging over the scene.

Just then, one of the marines gave a cry and fell to the ground, bleeding from a shoulder wound. While the medic attended him, Sten dragged the man's weapons pack over and started pawing through it, hoping Ida had supplied the Marines with a few of the nastier God Box weapons.

He breathed a sigh of relief when he found what he needed: a slender tube about half a meter long. He drew it out, twisted it, and the tube grew in girth until it was as thick as his arm.

Then he gave it a back and forth twist and pulled. The device telescoped out until it was a little over a meter-and-a-half long.

He turned to the weapons pack, but Mk'wolf had seen what he was up to and had dug out a bullet-shaped object about 25 centimeters long.

Sten took the device, gave the bottom a hard pediatrician-like slap, and three fins popped out. And after he inserted it into the tube, the device started to glow a rich golden color.

What he was holding in his hands now was a very deadly weapon—a *Fēidàn* Javelin. A kind of shoulder-fired missile said to have been first invented by the Chinese on Old Earth.

He turned back to the crane. "Get another one ready," he told Mk'wolf. Then he took careful aim.

A woman on the Himmenops squad saw what he was up to. The only defense against the *Fēidàn* was to pin the would-be attacker down with all the fire power you could muster and never let him up.

Sten hoped like clot her training had been negligent.

No such luck.

She shouted to her comrades and they all turned and opened up on Sten.

AM2 rounds whizzed all around him. But he held steady, bringing the *Fēidàn* to bear on the crane's boom.

He ran the sights down the jib until he came to the place where it joined the body of the machine. From his machine shop schooldays back on Vulcan he knew that's where the gravunits would be.

The AM2 fire became so heavy that it was all he could do to defy the instinct to duck before one of the rounds took his head off.

Then he depressed the trigger and—*whoosh!*—the *Fēidàn* streaked out, leaving a shower of sparks in its wake, as it shot toward the crane.

Compared to most weapons of its kind, the Javelin was agonizingly slow and wobbled in its course. The Himmenops turned their attention on the missile, blazing away.

But the *Fēidàn* jerked this way and that, automatically avoiding enemy fire. It was clumsy, but it worked.

And then the missile struck.

Flames gouted from the base of the crane.

A deafening explosion. Then another.

Smoke boiled up. And then there was a loud screech of metal ripping away.

And slowly, so slowly, the boom came down. It hit the warehouse floor with a resounding crash. Metal parts flew everywhere.

The cloud of dust it raised was too thick to make out much, but to Sten's enormous relief, when they cleared he saw the Himmenops women dashing back to safety. One of them was helping another, but other than that, it didn't look like anyone had been hurt too badly.

The marines cheered. Mk'wolf started to get up, ready to lead the marines in a charge, but Kilgour grabbed him and pulled him back while Sten motioned for the others to stay put.

He fiddled with his com unit, turning it to "Big Voice." Drew in several deep breaths. Composing himself.

Then he spoke up. "Venatora," he called out. His voice, magnified many times, boomed across the warehouse.

No answer.

"Venatora," he called out again. "I hope to clot you're there. We don't want anyone else to get hurt, do we?"

Still no answer.

He glanced over at Kilgour, who shook his head. "Nae a prayer's chance in perdition, laddie," he muttered.

But Sten didn't think Venatora was the sort who would let others do her fighting for her. She'd want to kill her own snakes.

With Sten, in this case, serving as the serpent.

He was about to shout her name again, when her voice rang

out. Clear and calm and without a hint of worry.

"Is that you, lieutenant?" she said. "The poor soldier with a hundred grand in ready money?"

CHAPTER EIGHTEEN

STEN AND VENATORA

Across the warehouse, Venatora's head popped into view. Several of her guardswomen hissed for her to get back under cover.

She ignored them.

"You didn't answer my question," she said, a smile twitching the corner of her lips. "Are you the poor soldier who somehow managed to scrape together a hundred grand for a wager?"

"Guilty as charged, my lady," Sten replied.

"Do you suppose you're up for another bet?" Venatora asked.

"Depends on the stakes," Sten said.

"How about your life?" Venatora said.

"Are you offering odds?" Sten asked.

"I might," Venatora said. "How are you powers of persuasion, Lieutenant?"

"Let's find out," Sten said.

And with that, he rose from cover. An AM2 round buzzed past. Sten didn't flinch.

"Get down," Mk'wolf, hissed. "She'll kill you."

Instead, Sten stepped from behind the barrier. "Here I am Venatora," he said. "Come out the rest of the way and we'll talk."

He scanned the far corner of the warehouse. Venatora had vanished. He saw a flash of metal. Then a spark. Another AM2 round buzzed past his head. Then he heard a loud flesh upon flesh smack.

A moment later, Venatora emerged.

Just the sight of her struck him a hard, breath-robbing blow. Like her guardswomen, Venatora's attire was minimal. A small, black halter top. Black modesty patch where her thighs joined. Black metal bands circling her wrists and biceps. Her figure was lush, ebony skin glowing in the harsh overhead lights.

There was something so primal about her it was all Sten could do to keep from rushing over to embrace her.

Almost as if hypnotized, he took a step forward. Then another. "Sten!" Kilgour barked.

With great difficulty, he stopped.

* * * *

Venatora watched Sten's struggle, mildly surprised at her own reaction. She wasn't displeased that he could resist her. In fact, she felt the thrill of challenge.

She increased her powers. Pheromones flowing from the special glands that were both her gift and her curse. Behind her, she heard low moans of lust from her women, who were similarly affected.

Sten took another step forward. Then another. She was almost disappointed. Even so, she increased her powers.

Then—to her delight—he stopped. She could tell that it was with great difficulty. But just the same he had the will to defy her siren musk.

She called out: "What do you want, Lieutenant?"

His reply was husky. Voice cracking. "You know."

She chuckled. "What are you offering?"

Sten shook his head. Helpless to answer. She thrilled when she saw him lift a foot, as if to take another step. To her dismay, he moved back. Just one step.

But that small bit of defiance shook her. She started to get angry.

"I could kill you," she said.

"I know," Sten said.

She increased her powers. Saw him quiver. Knew she almost had him. Then, to her amazement, he took one more step back.

"Wait!" she cried. Her voice a little shaky.

Sten came to halt.

"What do you want?" she asked.

"You know," he said again.

"To live?"

Sten laughed. It wasn't a forced laugh. But lusty. From the belly.

"For what I have in mind," he said, "life would be the minimum requirement."

Now it was Venatora's turn to laugh. "You're expecting a great deal," she said. "What would I have to gain?"

"Oh, I think you know," Sten said.

This time the sound of his voice thrilled her. She felt heat in her loins. She steeled herself. How was it that this…this…*human*… could affect her so?

She grew angry. "You killed my sisters," she said. "I could never forgive that."

"They attacked us," Sten said.

"They were just going to detain you," Venatora said. "They had strict order not to harm you."

"How was I to know?" Sten said. "You should have come yourself."

Venatora snorted derision. "I suppose you'd let me take you captive."

Sten shrugged. "We could have discussed it," he said.

"It's too late now," Venatora said. "Three of my people—my sisters—are dead."

Sten raised a hand, displaying two fingers. "Two," he said. "Not three." He paused, then added. "Would it help if I said I re-gretted those two?"

Venatora didn't reply.

Sten turned his head. She heard him say, "Bring her out."

With a start, she saw the heavy worlder friend of the lieutenant lead one of her women out. Her heart jumped.

It was Marta, by God!

The sergeant handed Marta over to Sten. She almost fell, but Sten steadied her, bearing her weight.

"She's hurt," Sten said. "We gave her medical attention, but she needs more."

"Bring her to me," Venatora said.

"Can we meet in the middle?" Sten asked. "If only to please my own people?"

Venatora hesitated, then nodded. "Very well," she said. "We'll declare a truce."

"Truce it is, then," Sten said. And started moving slowly for-ward, helping Marta along.

Venatora moved forward to meet him.

As she came closer, the atmosphere around her seemed to crackle with the sheer life force that was Venatora.

Sten's scalp prickled, and the hair on the back of his neck rose. He felt feverish, his mouth grew dry, his throat thick. He felt drawn to her like a powerful magnet.

The closer she came, the stronger the pull. And he had a sense that the attraction was as great for her. That she was being drawn to him by a mysterious force.

But then, when she was few meters away, she suddenly stopped. Sten almost groaned aloud. He could see that she was shaken as well.

Perspiration trickled down one perfect cheek.

They stood there in silence for a long time.

Finally, Venatora spoke, voice thick. "Who are you?"

"I told you. Sten. Lieutenant Sten."

"No. Really. Who are you?"

Sten shrugged. He had no other answer.

"One of my fathers said something like this might happen one day," Venatora said.

"What might happen?"

Venatora motioned, delicate hand indicating the two of them. "This."

Sten wondered what she meant by "one of my fathers." How many fathers could she have? But he said nothing.

"He said if it did, I should kill you without delay," Venatora added.

"I'm glad you didn't take his advice," Sten said.

"One of my other fathers disagreed," Venatora said.

"I'm happy to hear that," Sten said.

Venatora shrugged. "There's still time," she said.

Another long silence. Sten could almost see the wheels turning in Venatora's head.

With great force of will she made her decision.

"I'm here for Marta," she said.

Sten sighed. "So you are," he said.

He moved away from Marta, who wavered, then took a step forward. Sten gently pushed at the small of her back. She took another, then another, and then collapsed at Venatora's feet.

"Here, let me help," Sten said.

But Venatora raised a hand, stopping him. She signaled and two women ran forward, collected Marta, and carried her away.

Sten and Venatora were alone again. They looked each other over. Hungrily.

And Sten saw resolve firm in Venatora's eyes.

"Goodbye, Lieutenant Sten," she said and started away.

"What about next time?" Sten called after her. "What will you do then?"

Venatora paused, looking back at him over her shoulder. Sten thought he had never seen a woman so woman so beautiful—so desirable.

"Kill you," she said.

CHAPTER NINETEEN

FLIGHT FROM PORT CHINEN

The warrior women hustled Venatora along a warren of tunnels, alleyways, and abandoned buildings to a rooftop where transport to her ship waited. She resisted when they tried to push her on board and insisted that the medics deal with Marta first. Then she got in and told her pilot to wait while she sussed things out.

Across the chaos that was Port Chinen, she saw the immense black gates that marked the Imperial fortress. Security bots armed with missiles swooped overhead, on constant alert for any outside danger. It was an open secret that the fortress was ringed with enough armament and trained personnel to hold off even a large force. But as she examined the imposing edifice, she noted cracks in the security she'd make use of one day.

Venatora had designs on Port Chinen. She'd even made informal contacts with the Tahn, a new enemy of the Eternal Emperor, whose support would be priceless when she made the fortress her own.

The Tahn were a chilly people. An obsessively warlike people. But Venatora was secure in her redoubt deep in the Possnet Sector and had little to fear from their notorious backstabbing ways.

Meanwhile, she'd have to be patient until she had the means to expand her hive and establish new ones.

But that would have to wait until she closed the deal with the mutineers and got her hands on all that Imperium X.

Yes, she would have to be patient, an increasingly difficult task. The pressures for expansion were enormous. There were more princesses—queens in waiting—than at any other time in her reign. Most were easily malleable, but there more than a few chafed for hives of their own, or plotted her overthrow.

Her assassins had dealt with the worst of the lot, and her network of spies kept sharp eyes on the others. But she had to be careful. If she went too far—killed too many, or clamped down too hard—the hive would become so restive that her leadership skills, and her arsenal of pheromonic weapons, might not be enough to retain control. Civil war, then chaos, then anarchy would surely follow. Her fathers had warned her again and again what to expect.

The Emperor's space-train of Imperium X would put paid to all those problems. And more. Nightmares of collapsed hives would be replaced with dreams of a glorious, ever expanding domain.

That, in short, was her dilemma. Certain failure. Or success beyond her wildest dreams. There was no in-between.

And Sten was the key to it all. She wished she didn't have to kill him. But at present she could see no other way.

As she kept watch on the fortress, she spotted a contingent of Imperial gravcars speeding up to the gates. Several security bots swooped down to sniff the vehicles out, gave them the all-clear, and a minute later the big gates groaned open.

She guessed that one of them contained Sten, who would be in a hurry after his encounter with her to make his case with the mutineers.

Venatora was about to give her pilot the go-ahead when the implanted com unit buzzed in her ear.

She tapped her throat-mic. "Yes, Father Raggio?" she said.

The buzzing resumed. It was a shorthand developed by her fathers to communicate quickly and concisely no matter where she was.

When it ended she said, "I'm sorry I was unable to carry out your orders, Father Raggio. I'll soon remedy that. Sten will be dead, as ordered, the first opening I get."

More buzzing. She frowned. Then: "You're happy it turned out that way? But why?"

She listened intently. A look of confusion on her face. "Yes, Father Raggio," she said. "I understand all that. But what if—"

Again, buzzing cut her off. Now, she looked really confused.

"I confess that he did affect me that way," she replied when he was done. "But I can control that. You know I can."

More buzzing. More listening. Finally, she smiled.

"Oh, I understand what you are getting at," she said. "Very clever. But do all the other fathers agree?"

What she heard next made her laugh. "Even Father Huber? Well, that has to be a first."

More laughter. Then Father Raggio signed off.

Venatora settled back into her seat. For the first time since she met Sten at the Xypaca fight, she felt at ease.

Then, for no apparent reason, she started getting angry.

"Well, clot him!" she said, startling the others. "Clot Sten all to hell!"

And then she brusquely ordered the pilot to get underway.

CHAPTER TWENTY

THE ETERNAL EMPEROR

It was a beautiful spring day on Prime World, and when Mahoney strolled through the Emperor's private garden, he was delighted see it was in full bloom. The colors and perfume of the exotic flowers and plants teased the eye and excited the senses.

There was a hint of wood smoke on the air, and when Mahoney rounded the lemon tree, its branches weighed down with ripening fruit, he found the Emperor bustling about his outdoor kitchen, directing several little bots to deposit the ingredients for the meal he was preparing on a long, rough wood table.

"Ah, Ian," he said, "you're just in time for my daily 'those sons of bitches' session. You do the honors with the booze while I get the Aubergine Politiko ready for the oven."

Chuckling, Mahoney made his way to the portable bar, set up near a beehive-shaped brick oven. A ribbon of mesquite smoke rose from the chimney.

"So, we're roasting politicians today, are we boss?" he said.

The Emperor snorted. "Ian, if I get much more lip from those scrotes in Parliament, don't be surprised if I have the whole lot of them drawn and quartered and fed to the pigs."

"We don't have any pigs handy, Sir," Ian said, "but give me a couple of hours and I'll have a grav-truck load ready and waiting at the gates."

He reached for the Scotch, but the Emperor stopped him. "Let's start with ouzo, Ian," he said. "We're celebrating the Greeks today."

"Any special reason, boss?" Mahoney asked, guessing correctly that a bit of informality would be welcome.

The Emperor ran his French knife through a large purple vegetable, cutting it lengthwise into thin slices. Grabbed another, and did the same.

"I'm trying to remind myself why I chose democracy back when I set up this whole shebang," the Emperor said, "instead of something sensible, like a dictatorship."

Mahoney nodded, then found a clear liquid in a bottle marked "ouzo." He fetched it down from the shelf.

"Let's face it," the Emperor continued, "strongman rule is lot more efficient. There is no pretense of consulting anyone. You just do it. If anybody complains, you toss them into the slammer."

He waved the knife. "And if that didn't work, my less sensitive brothers and sisters of tyranny just cut out their tongues."

He was smiling when he said the last, so Mahoney chuckled. He wasn't always sure when his boss was joking, but at the moment it seemed a safe enough assumption. Even so, his tongue suddenly felt a little larger in his mouth.

The Emperor held up one of the purple vegetables. "You see this?"

Mahoney nodded. "I see it, boss, but I don't have the faintest idea what it is."

"Its fancy name is Aubergine," he said. "But in reality it's only a clotting eggplant."

"Gotcha, boss," Mahoney said, pouring a couple of fingers of ouzo into two glasses.

The clear liquid turned cloudy when he added a couple of ice cubes and a splash of water. He set one before the Emperor and took a sip of his own. Ouzo tasted like licorice—not one of Ian's favorite flavors—but like most booze, after a couple of pops, it went down just fine.

"Same with democracy," the Emperor said. "Just a fancy word invented by the Greeks for a political system that is always bordering on chaos and outright anarchy."

He started the eggplant strips frying in olive oil, then set to work dicing blood-red tomatoes fresh from his garden.

"Of course, it wasn't a real democracy," he said. "Even in Athens there were more slaves than citizens. And to be fair, it was the rich families who ran things, not your average Joe Papadopoulos."

Mahoney thought that it sounded pretty much like how things were today. Even here on Prime World, where the Emperor took a personal interest in government, it was the rich and well-connected who had the upper hand. Elsewhere in the Empire, his boss maintained a general hands-off policy. As long as they paid their AM2 bills on time and didn't conspire with his enemies, he let them run things pretty much the way they wanted. But if they crossed him—well, that's when he sent for Mahoney. Which is why, Ian strongly suspected, the Emperor had invited him to dinner.

The Emperor said, "You know, after being the Man in Charge for a couple of millennia or so, you'd think I'd get used to those guys in Parliament. It goes without saying that they are all greedy backstabbers—that's the nature of the beast."

He sipped his ouzo. Nodded appreciatively.

"Bet if I commissioned a study from one of my pet eggheads," he continued, "they'd find that a whopping majority of the drakh-heads were abused as children. Which is why they become politicians. To revenge themselves on an uncaring world."

"I wouldn't take that bet, boss," Ian said. "Never met a politico whose headbolts weren't on just finger tight."

The Emperor laughed. Using his broad-bladed knife, he swept the diced tomatoes into a bowl, then got busy mincing a half a dozen or so fat garlic bulbs, followed by a palmful of basil. The scent soon had Mahoney's mouth watering.

Drakh the politicians. He was hungry.

"Normally I take everything in stride," the Emperor said. "I have my little tricks, you know?"

He paused to polish off his ouzo and slid the empty glass over to Ian, who downed his own and made a couple of fresh drinks.

"Like this dish," the Emperor said. "Different ingredients that might not always play well together in your belly. But if I assemble them just so…"

He grabbed the pan of sizzling eggplant and layered it in a baking dish. Then he quickly spooned the mixture of tomatoes, garlic and basil on the eggplant and blessed the contents with a few twists of sea salt and a couple of cranks of black pepper.

The Emperor displayed the contents to Ian. "Looks a mess, doesn't it?" he said. "Just a jumble of veggies that'll slop off your plate. But then I do this…"

He got out a big bowl of what Ian took to be some sort of crumbled white cheese.

"Feta," the Emperor said. "Goat's cheese."

Mahoney frowned. He'd tried goat before. It was during a barely remembered foray against a nomadic desert tribe. The ripe smell of old goat meat roasting over a dried dung fire brought the memory back, and he wrinkled his nose.

The Emperor caught his reaction. Laughed. Shoved the bowl at Ian. "Give it a try," he said.

Ian hesitated. "Go on," the Emperor pressed. "You'll be surprised."

Mahoney took a pinch of cheese and popped it into mouth. To his delight, the flavor was neither strong nor mild, but smooth and mellow with just a little bite at the back of the tongue.

The Emperor smiled at Mahoney's pleased expression.

"Most folks think there are only four flavors," the Emperor said. "Sweet, bitter, sour and salty. But my daddy taught me that there was a fifth. He called it Umami. Said it made your taste buds complete."

He tapped the bowl. "Like this feta cheese," he said.

With that, the Emperor grabbed up a double handful of feta and distributed it over the eggplant mixture. He repeated the action until the baking dish wore a snow-white cap of cheese.

Then he washed his hands, donned some fireproof gloves and moved to the oven. He slid the dish onto a metal rack on one side.

"When that's done," the Emperor said, "I'll have turned an unruly mess into something not only manageable, but delicious. All because I played dictator and imposed my culinary will on chaos."

Although his boss was speaking in vague generalities, Ian was starting to get the feeling that the Emperor had it in for somebody in particular, and he started running down a mental list of potential candidates for the high jump.

But he forgot all that when the Emperor reached back into the oven and pulled out a sizzling roasting-tray and the tantalizing odor of chicken and lemon and spices filled the air.

His boss placed the tray on the table, revealing a large, golden brown chicken surrounded by quarter-cut, unpeeled potatoes, also a rich brown.

He flipped the chicken over—breast side down—and stirred the potatoes, exposing the underdone white surfaces. He spooned chicken gravy over the whole thing.

Mahoney had enjoyed this dish once before. It was Greek lemon chicken and potatoes. He knew the Emperor had rubbed the chicken inside and out with mixture of lemon—fresh from the tree in his garden—extra virgin olive oil, Greek oregano, and minced garlic. The potatoes got a similar bath.

The Emperor put the pan back in the oven and turned to Ian, stripping off the gloves. Ian dutifully started to pour a couple of more ouzos, but the Emperor raised a hand.

"We're going to need something stronger about now, Ian," he said. "Metaxa should do the trick."

Mahoney smiled. "Metaxa, it is, boss."

This drink went straight to Ian's Irish heart. It was an ancient Greek liqueur—a mixture of brandy and wine—the Emperor had spent decades recreating. It had a flavor like no other, and had a way of boosting your energy and mental faculties. Very much like Irish whiskey, but without the resultant hangover.

They both downed a couple of shots, then Mahoney refilled their glasses. They would sip these while the Emperor made a Greek salad—mainly greens from his garden with a goat cheese, lemon, and olive oil dressing.

While he worked his knife, the Emperor said, "I assume you heard that Lord Wichman is considering a run for president of the Parliament."

Mahoney's eyes narrowed. So that's what this was about.

"He's formed one of those phony exploratory committees," the Emperor continued. "You know, where they get a group of people together to discuss a decision that's already been made."

Mahoney grimaced. "When it comes to politics, Wichman's a joke," he said. "He bought his seat in Parliament I don't know how many years ago. From what I've heard, nobody has seen him on the floor since he was sworn in."

"Well, he's been a busy boy since his son got himself taken hostage," the Emperor continued. "Seems he's greased enough palms to buy a seat on the Special Select Intelligence Committee."

Ian's eyebrows rose. The few beings who knew anything about the mutiny were on that panel. Mahoney had dealt with the members on and off over the years—usually around budget time. Normally, they were all handpicked by the Emperor for their ability to keep their mouths shut and increase Mercury Corps funding whenever the Emperor—at Ian's behest—deemed it necessary.

Apparently Wichman had managed to bypass the Emperor's control of the panel.

Mahoney said, "Let me take a wild guess, Your Highness. He's threatening to leak news about the mutiny to force us to take immediate action to free his son."

The Emperor sighed. "Not to my face," he said. "Or to the faces of any of my representatives. Otherwise we wouldn't be having this oh-so-reasonable conversation over a nice Greek dinner."

Mahoney nodded. An open threat by Wichman would have brought the Emperor's wrath down upon him.

"Doesn't he know that if we move on the mutineers, the first casualty will be his son?" Mahoney said.

The Emperor snorted. "He doesn't give a drakh about his son," he said. "Probably worth more to him martyred than alive. He'd be a shoo-in for the presidency of the Parliament."

The light suddenly dawned for Mahoney. "And the presidency would give him a seat at the table in any negotiations with the Tahn," he said. The picture became clearer still. "He's got visions of trading up from casinos and resorts to some serious war profiteering."

The Emperor roared laughter and clapped him on the back. "Give that man a cee-gar," he said. Patted his breast pocket. "Fresh out," he said. "Filthy habit, anyway."

So he poured them both two more Metaxas instead.

"What do you want to do about him, boss?" Mahoney said.

"Right now, nothing," the Emperor replied. "In fact, I'm going to buddy up to him as if I don't suspect a thing. We're even going to grant him a favor. Which I need you for."

"Yes, sir?"

"He wants a way to communicate with his son without the mutineers knowing about it," the Emperor said.

Ian thought a minute, then nodded. "I can have Lieutenant Sten try to slip Gregor something when he's aboard the *Flame*, negotiating with the mutineers."

"Will we be able to monitor what is said?" the Emperor wanted to know.

"No problem, boss."

"Then, do it," the Emperor said.

"Uh...boss... One other thing?"

"Yes?"

"Do we still want to keep Gregor alive, sir? I mean, now that we know his daddy doesn't really care all that much."

"Nothing's changed, Ian," the Emperor said. "In fact, tell young Sten that if something bad happens to Gregor you'll bust him down to whatever is lower than a buck private."

"Yessir."

"Good. Now let's eat."

And he went to oven and hauled out his dish of the day: Aubergine Politiko.

A minute later, Mahoney and the Eternal Emperor were digging in with gusto.

But at the back of his mind Mahoney couldn't help but wonder what special kind of Hell the Emperor had in mind for Lord Wichman.

CHAPTER TWENTY ONE

THE NAVIGATOR

The congregation of the Church of the Universal Location sat hunched over their holo boards, crystalline light wands flickering as they built a wondrous image.

Swirling numbers and symbols cometed across uttermost space, leaving glowing trails and bursts of light as miniature suns bloomed, then died; planets were ripped from orbit and thrown into one another, shattering into a great sparkling clouds of rock and ice and dust.

In the center of the group—directing the congregation like an orchestra maestro—was the dark, slender figure of Bishop Shaklin, waving arms elegantly to the rhythm of inner music, beaded dreadlocks clacking, keeping time.

As exotic and complex as the slowly developing scene on the Holoimager appeared, Shaklin devoted only a small part of his brain on the group's mutual task: navigating the tricky shoals of the Possnet Sector.

It was a desolate place, created by a billion-year-old disaster. It was like the island chains on ancient Earth, where continental shelves collided and volcanoes erupted on the floor of the seas, dribbling out land masses in the form of molten lava.

And like the islands, the desolate mini-worlds of Possnet Sector were inhabited by beings who had fled famine and pestilence and the wrath of others.

It was an ideal "Hole in the Wall" for criminals and terrorists and pirates like Venatora and her Himmenops.

They were by far the most powerful and feared of the Possnet pirates and if Venatora drew Aces in her deadly game for the Emperor's Imperium X she would rival the Eternal Emperor himself out here in the Fringe Worlds.

And if he tried to send the Imperial Navy in after her, the Emperor's losses would be enormous.

The *Flame* sat on the very edge of her domain. Shaklin jabbed his wand at one section, and a red light started flashing. Directing his congregation to follow his lead, he waved his wand, and more red lights popped up.

Some of the lights represented Venatora's fortresses, all defended by her Zabanya guardswomen. Most were mine fields carefully laid out to confound even the most sophisticated battle computers.

The mines were the best money could buy on the arms black market and were quite capable of taking out an Imperial battleship if an overconfident ship's captain became careless.

Venatora had been pressing the mutineers to conclude the deal. Zheng and Rual were all but convinced, especially as the anxiety level of the other crewmembers rose to the boiling point.

Still, Shaklin urged patience. He appealed to the greed of Zheng and Rual, pointing out that the Emperor could easily outbid Venatora and there was no reason to believe that he'd ever let all that Imperium X loose on the black market.

Shaklin, however, was mainly concerned about what kind of lonely existence they were all in for if they had to take refuge in the Possnet Sector for the rest of their lives.

"We can never leave," he told them. "The Emperor will have a price on all our heads. Why, some of the other pirates might even be tempted to betray us to the Imperials."

"The clottin' Emperor will never give us amnesty," Rual insisted during one heated discussion.

Rual was starting to get over-excited, pacing up and down, waving her arms. "And even if he does agree, how do we know he'll keep his word?"

Shaklin knew that much of Rual's reluctance was that she wanted avenge herself on Gregor. He had some sympathy with that view, although violence was abhorrent to all members of the Church of the Universal Location.

At the perfect intersection of locus points there would be eternal peace and plenty for all beings who dared travel the soul-wearying path of enlightenment. He and his people had been on that long journey as far as anyone could remember.

In the distant past, of which there were only oral records—tales told on wintery nights—his people had always been on that Road to Salvation. Be it across desert wastes, briny seas, steaming jungles, or bitterly cold and dark Uttermost Space.

No, he would avoid violence—unless it was absolutely necessary to protect himself and his congregation.

Besides, he doubted they could trust either one of them. When it came lies and betrayal, he suspected the Eternal Emperor and the Pirate Queen were equals.

And it was for this reason that Shaklin was desperately seeking a third way.

He and his congregation had been swept up in the mutiny. Gregor was a cruel master, and it was a wonder his throat hadn't been cut long before.

And so the congregation had rioted and mutinied with the others. Shaklin was ashamed to admit they had allowed greed to color their dreams as much as the others.

Dreams of enough credits to free themselves from all duties except the search for the Universal Location.

The Elders had been predicting a breakthrough for several decades now. Shaklin wondered—no, he prayed—that this mutiny would turn out to be a nugget of luck that would fund that final breakthrough to The Other.

But then reality had set in. And the viciousness of some of their fellow crewmembers—especially the ringleaders, Zheng and Rual—was appalling.

Once he'd recovered his senses, Shaklin started to plot another course. They would have to go along with the negotiations. Buying time to find another path.

There was a small escape craft on the *Flame* that Shaklin had been secretly rigging for a long jump. They would need supplies. And, yes, as much as he abhorred the idea, they would need weapons as well.

In the game between Venatora and the Emperor, there was sure to be a moment of maximum confusion when he and his congregation could slip away.

And the next thing anyone knew, they'd be gone.

Shaklin smiled to himself. He might even find a way to take a few of the ore cars with them. These could be sold for enough to fund years of travel and research.

Just then—on the far edge of swirling image—he saw a blip. Just a drop of golden light.

There it was again.

And again.

Then it was gone.

Shaklin turned his head. Across the chamber, Zheng was slumped in a gravchair, while Rual nervously paced back and forth.

Every once in awhile Zheng would take a surreptitious nip from a silver flask, his pink tongue darting in to lap up the spirits.

Rual's long, skeletal face seemed more drawn than usual. And her huge, never-blinking eyes seemed to stare into nothingness.

There was another blip on the Holoimager.

A drop of gold that appeared and then vanished so quickly you wondered if it was imaginary.

And then it came again, and Shaklin looked over at Zheng.

Rual, who could never stay still for a second, saw him turn.

She elbowed Zheng. Zheng looked up—expectant. Struggling to hide sudden fear.

And Shaklin mouthed the words, "They're coming."

CHAPTER TWENTY TWO

THE GANG OF THREE

Sten emptied the *Flame's* control room of everyone except his team to plan the vital first moves in their mission. The last thing they needed was interference from Capt. W'lson.

As Alex so aptly put it: "Th' captain is sae thick he cooldn't puir piss in a boot wi' a hole in th' toe an' th' directions writ oan th' heel."

As the team's psy-war expert, Doc took the lead. He had Shaklin's dossier up on the monitor. The bishop made an exotic figure with his long, beaded dreadlocks, wispy chin beard and dark, hawklike features.

"He's the greatest unknown," Doc said. "A True Believer. And if there was anything in this incarnation more dangerous than a True Believer, they'd weaponize it."

"What exactly do those clots believe in?" Ida asked. "And do we care?"

"As near as I can tell, after skimming over this drakh," Doc said, indicating a research fiche, "The Church of the Universal Location is sort of like Celestial Acupuncture. They do elaborate calculations—accompanied by all kinds of ceremonial garbage native to their culture—to determine so-called perfect locations in the Universe."

Sten's eyebrows rose. "Perfect," he said. "I've never heard of anything that was perfect."

Doc made a rude noise. "No drakh," he said. "Especially since they are human. There are few species less perfect than homo clotting sapiens."

Kilgour started to protest, but Sten shot him a warning look. It was no time to get into a squabble with Doc.

Doc continued. "What makes them 'perfect' escapes me. I'm

sure there is some imagined deity behind it all. There usually is. But so far I haven't found a mention of the clot's holy name. More than likely it is forbidden to say it aloud, or even write it down."

Doc gave a weary sigh. Fished out a bottle of his favorite hemo tonic—the blood of some poor critter native to home planet, Ceres III, that his kind had hunted to near extinction. The little bottle had probably cost him a small fortune. He took a long swig. Smacked his lips. Then returned to the subject at hand.

"Naturally," he said, "there is one location more perfect than all others." He shrugged. "Heaven, if you will."

"I clottin' will not," Ida said. "If there's a clottin' Heaven, there's has to be a Hell. And if there's a Hell, I am in deep, deep drakh." She snorted. "And here I am, barely into my third decade of so-called life and bound for Hell. So, let's leave clottin' heaven, and freakin' Hell out of the discussion, if you don't mind."

Sten laughed. "You know, Doc," he said, "your description of this religion sounds like a never-ending search for bumps in space. More like celestial phrenology than acupuncture."

Alex shook his head in mock sorrow. "Ach, to the likes of me it 'pears thae back afore th' Stone Age, some puir mammy must've dropped her wee bairn on its head."

Doc waved a furry little paw and Shaklin's dossier vanished. A split screen popped up showing Zheng and Rual.

Alex grimaced. "Thae Zheng bugger looks like a bloody toad," he said. "Guid fur clottin' naethin' but huntin' flies."

"Don't let his looks fool you," Doc said. "He's been in and out of prison half his life. Wanted in a dozen places all over the Empire."

"What for?" Sten asked.

"Zheng specializes in kidnapping," Doc said. "He started with someone's child when he was barely a child himself. Then he grad- uated to gravbus loads of tourists. He was never above killing a few hostages to hurry things along, so he was fairly successful— until it all caught to him and he had to flee. The Maritime Service made a wonderful hiding place."

Sten shook his head. He'd heard tales about the low standards in the Imperial merchant fleet, but he had no idea that wanted crim- inals could clog dance past Personnel into responsible shipboard positions.

"Well, now Zheng's gone and kidnapped himself a whole clotting space-train," Ida said. "No more small stuff."

"What about her?" Sten said, indicating Rual. "Does she have a criminal background as well?"

Doc shrugged. "Nothing like Zheng. Her offenses were mainly for—quote…grievous bodily assault and maiming…end quote… plus an unproven murder or three. She's got a temper and a long knife always at the ready."

Doc chuckled. Sten had noted over time that few things gave their resident shrink greater pleasure than discussing psychopaths. The more murderous, the more blood spilled, the better.

As if stirred by thoughts of all that flowing hemoglobin, Doc sighed wistfully, then took another hit off his bottle of hemo.

"Apparently she is an addicted gambler," he continued. "And a dangerously sore loser. She'll do anything—and I stress *any-thing*—to feed that habit. Lie, rob, even kill. It is my educated guess that her compulsion—and inability to handle loss—made her an ideal target for the machinations of Mutineer Number Three: Sr. Zheng."

Doc waved a paw and the three all appeared together, with Zheng in the center.

"In summary," Doc said, "Zheng's a born leader. He's a superior organizer. A master at defusing, or creating conflict among his crew members—whichever serves his purpose. Supporting all that, he has the ability to choose a goal and then stick with it at all cost."

He indicated Rual. "She's a born follower. Intensely loyal. Murderously volatile, so she probably has the other mutineers urinating in their under garments whenever her temper explodes. It's my prog that Zheng has her on a short leash, which he's likely to let loose if anyone crosses him. Naturally, this not only keeps the crew under his thumb—or her knife—but they probably admire him more. Foolishly arousing their trust in his ability to negotiate for them."

Sten shook his head. "Talk about a recipe for disaster," he said.

"There it is," Doc said. "Plus, we must keep in mind that Zheng is under tremendous pressure. If one thing goes wrong, the crew will turn on him, and even Rual won't be able to stop them. He's in hurry to make a deal and get as far away from the others as he can."

"So, he'll be wanting safe passage," Sten said, "as well as amnesty."

"Count on it," Doc said.

"Which brings us back to Shaklin," Sten said.

"Yes, Shaklin," Doc said. "He's both their weakest link and their strongest link. Weak because money is the least of his motives for joining the mutiny. One of our snitches back at Chinen reported that he holds Gregor responsible for the death of his lover, Pegatha. Sten's favorite scrote's habit of skimping on repairs and pocketing the money led to equipment failure at a crucial time, killing her."

He glanced at his report, then looked up and smacked his lips with unseemly gusto. Unseemly for anyone except a fellow Blyrchynaus, that is. "I understand it was a rather messy accident. Blood and gore everywhere."

Sten pushed past the sick feeling that Doc's habits sometimes aroused in him. "In other words," he said, "without the death of Pegatha, he might not have joined the mutiny."

"Exactly," Doc said. "And without Shaklin the mutiny would failed before it even began. Making him their strongest link. Because without his navigating and pilot skills, the mutineers have no bargaining power. One false move by an opponent and he'll jump the *Flame*, cargo train and all, to the other side of the Empire."

With that bit of intel, light dawned for them.

Sten said, "Otherwise Venatora would have boarded their ship long ago, cut their throats, and made off with the cargo."

"Who would't think sech a bony lass hae so much murder in her breast?" Alex mourned.

Sten thought about his last meeting with Venatora. Yes, he'd seen murder glittering in her eyes. But also something else. Something…

He shivered and forced himself back to the present.

But Ida caught it. "Wet dreaming about your lady love, are you dear?" she purred.

With great difficulty, Sten ignored her. "I think Mahoney's first idea still holds," he said. "We push them. Gently. But firmly. See how they react. Make them nervous. Then we throw them an olive branch."

"Wi' a bester grenade attached," Kilgour said.

Sten sighed. As usual, Alex was spot on. Then he braced himself and sent word to Captain W'lson.

It was time to bring the crew and officers of the *Flame* up to date. And it would take all his newly won skills at diplomacy—Mantis style—to bring it off.

CHAPTER TWENTY THREE

INVITATION TO A STEW POT

"To start with," Sten said, "we're going to put the frighteners on them. If we do it right, when we pop up on their vid there won't be a clean pair of skivvies on the ship."

His eyes swept over the faces of the assembled officers of the *Jo'l Cash*, pausing just long enough to look into the eyes of each to make sure he had their full attention.

He stopped at Captain W'lson, who was clearly uncomfortable in a subordinate role. Beside her, Mk'wolf was paying close attention to Sten's every word.

"But here's the main thing," Sten continued. "Yes, we want spook them. But not so much that they take to their heels."

W'lson frowned. "But if they run," she said, "We need to be ready to give chase. We can't give them time to jump."

Behind him, Sten heard Alex mutter a curse—but in a brogue so thick that W'lson was unlikely to take offense if she heard it.

"Negative," Sten said. "First off, we have to keep in mind that we have their navigators to deal with."

W'lson snorted derision. "They're just merchantmen," she said. "What kind of training can they have? Nothing to compare to our people, who are graduates of the Imperial Navy's navigation school."

"If we underestimate our enemy," Sten said, "the game will be lost before we begin. We're not talking about ordinary navigators, you know. These beings are most likely as good as—and maybe even better than—any ship drivers in the Imperial Navy. If we go scrotes to the wall and just charge the *Flame*, Shaklin will jump the ship to the other end of the Possnet Sector faster than an Altarian spider strike. And we can say goodbye to any kind of a deal and hello to Queen Venatora."

He fixed W'lson with a hard stare. "And while you are it, say goodbye to your career because the Emperor will have your guts for a winding sheet."

But W'lson was a stubborn clot. An old line officer who couldn't get over her resentment of having to take orders from a much younger person.

"How do you know they won't just run, then?" she said. "We go boo and they do a million-klick jump. What's to stop them?"

Something his father had told him flashed into Sten's mind. It was about a strange little pest that gorged on his old man's crops back on his homeworld. This was back before he and Sten's mom had sold their souls to the Vulcan Factory Store.

And in that memory Sten sensed opportunity.

Sten knew the session with W'lson and the other officers was being vidded throughout the entire ship. And that many of the many crewmembers aboard the *Jo 'l Cash*—especially out here on the fringes of the Empire—were more than likely ex farmkids, just like his dad.

He perched on a counter edge, putting himself and—he hoped—the whole ship—at ease.

"My old man grew up in the boonies," Sten said. "Farmboy. Sharecropper's kid. Knew what it was like to stare up the butt of a tractor drone so old and rusted out that half the time you had to push it by hand across the field."

He saw smiles on the faces of Mk'wolf and a few of the other officers. He'd sussed his audience correctly.

"What Dad remembered most was being hungry. Belly pinch your backbone hungry. Clottin' farmlords took ninety clottin' percent of the crops."

There were nods from Mk'wolf and the others. They knew what he was talking about.

"So Dad was always on the lookout for something to catch for the family pot."

Sten paused. A reflective smile twitched his lips. "His mom had this big stew pot—probably so old it was made out of iron— hanging over an actual fire. They used methane piped in from the drakh pits for fuel."

He shook his head in admiration of that old pioneer stock. Then he went on:

"The old man said there was this one critter—it was small and furry and a champion babymaker. They could eat a sharecropping family out of house and hut in a single planetfall. Lepus, I think he called them. Anyway, my old man figured what's fair is fair and if these little bassids were getting fat from eating his family's crops, why he'd find a way to eat them. Turn that stolen fat into some kind of use.

"So he'd hunt the little suckers. Every morning he'd fill his pockets with rocks and take a stroll along the field. Find himself a Lepus trail—their drakh gives them away...eat so much they're always poopin'."

Mk'wolf snickered. He'd been there.

"Pop said that the problem was the beasties had a sixth sense for danger. You'd barely lay eyes on them and they'd take off. And fast—why, he said they were faster than a cat runnin' from a corn rat.

Sten sighed, shaking his head at the memory. "At first my old man thought they had him beat," she said. "No way could he chase them down. But then he saw that they'd only hop like hell for ten, fifteen meters or so. Then they'd stop. Look back to see if you had given up the chase."

Sten shrugged. "Guess a lot of other critters did just that. They'd see how fast a Lepus could hop and they'd give up practically before they started. Throw up their paws and go, oh drakh, and look for some nice non-hopping berries to munch on."

Some of the officers laughed. W'lson glowered at them, but they paid her no mind.

Sten continued: "But Dad saw that the Lepus were both lazy and curious at the same time. They didn't want to put out all that much energy. Plus, they wanted to see what the clot you were up to.

"So, they'd plump down and wait. If you ran after them again, they'd take to their heels and off they'd go. They'd let you spend all day, stopping and starting until the day was over and your mom was calling you to supper. If there was even going to be supper, that is."

The pretty young lieutenant next to Mk'wolf frowned at this, shaking her head. Sten guessed that she'd known what it was like to go to bed hungry.

"But my old man was determined to fill that stewpot no matter what," Sten said. "So he started studying on the Lepus. He'd run a few steps. They'd hop a couple of hops. Until, little by little he'd only be maybe ten meters away."

Mk'wolf laughed. "Until he was in rock range," he blurted. Then he blushed like a kid for speaking out of turn.

Sten laughed, as did the others. "Until he was in rock range," he repeated. "He kept one clutched in his hand just waiting his chance. And when the right time came—"

He pivoted, then sidearmed an imaginary rock. Hard!

"And, *bam!* He had him a Lepus for the stew pot. First day he got half a dozen and his family ate like farmlords."

The payoff was greeted with laughter and applause—as if everybody had been enjoying a viddie, instead of yawning over a headache-inducing lecture from the Big Man in Charge.

Sten let everyone have a good laugh and chatter amongst themselves for a few minutes, then came off the bench. He stood ramrod straight.

"Except, we're going to go one better," Sten said. "We're gonna give them a choice.

He held up a clenched fist.

"A rock."

Sten let the hand drop. Gave them a big grin.

"Or, they can climb into the stewpot themselves."

As if on cue, Alex came in: "Ah'll wager our Sten'll hae them beggin' fur th' salt an' pepper."

Laughter, then Ida called out:

"Got a visual!"

CHAPTER TWENTY FOUR

CAT AND MOUSE

The bright yellow blip on Shaklin's Holoimager held steady for a measured beat, then bloomed, unfolding like a blossom.

He glanced over at Viktor and Newton, the two most experienced members of the group. Both gave him the high sign.

Shaklin nodded agreement. "Stations, everyone," he said.

Immediately, his congregants tucked away their crystal wands and took up position around the specially designed navcenter.

From here they could keep track of every point in the Possnet Sector, as well as countless jump points ranging from several hundred thousands of kilometers, to distances many light years away.

They were also in control of both the ship's McLean generators and AM2 drives. Everything else came under the control of Zheng and Rual at the Command Board, including the weapons systems.

Shaklin was uncomfortable with that part of the arrangement, but there was nothing he could say or do to change it without arousing suspicion.

Still, having Rual so close to the guns was frightening.

The yellow blip that was the *Jo'l Cash* suddenly brightened and shot forward.

Rual shouted in alarm, "They're coming! They're coming!"

Shaklin ignored her, but moved a hand over the drive panel. A double tap brought up the jump choices. A single tap would send the *Flame* and the 125-kilometer space-train in any direction he chose.

But that option would only be used as a last resort.

The yellow blip kept advancing, and Rual was jumping up and down and screaming, *"Jump! Jump! What's wrong with you? Jump!"*

But Shaklin held his nerve and didn't budge a micron.

The blip gave another surge and Rual ran at him, shouting, "Run! Run! We *gotta* run!"

Shaklin turned his head and fixed Rual with a glare so fierce it stopped her in her tracks. And she hung there, while Shaklin calmly turned back to his controls and goosed the McLean generator a bit. The *Flame* moved away from the *Jo'l Cash*—swiftly, but hardly at top speed.

Just as he suspected, the *Jo'l Cash* suddenly stopped. So that was their game, was it? Cat and mouse.

So he stopped as well, bringing a groan from Rual who was desperate to do something—anything. Zheng leaned in and whispered something to her, but it seemed to have little effect.

A few heartbeats later the *Jo'l Cash* shot forward again. And once again Shaklin goosed the McLean generator, retreating, then stopping when the *Jo'l Cash* pulled up.

The maneuver was repeated several more times. Now Rual and Zheng were hanging behind him watching the whole thing in a daze.

Then there was a change. The *Jo'l Cash* was on the move again, but this time when it stopped a silver cloud floated from ports in the nose. The image of the cloud glittered across the Holoimager, flowing out toward the *Flame*.

"Vhat's dat?" Zheng muttered. "Particles, they look like."

And then the cloud enveloped their ship, passing over and around it. The only apparent effect was the sound of scratching, like sand blowing across a faceplate. And then it was gone.

"They're clottin' painting us," Rual said, her voice quivering. "We'll have a missile up our butts next."

Shaklin double checked his instruments. No sign of any danger that he could see. And if they fired, he could still beat them to the punch.

Even so, he was getting nervous. It was difficult to keep his cool with Rual on an emotional razor's edge.

His hand moved to hover over the Jump panel. Rual and Zheng were talking, but he couldn't make out what they were saying.

The pressure was getting to him. He felt otherworldly, with Zheng and Rual moving their lips, but he couldn't make out a word.

Maybe they were right. Maybe he should end this game and jump.

Yes, jump, he thought. Enough of this nonsense. Better jump.

But before he could act, a voice boomed through their com units.

"This is Captain Sten, aboard the *Jo 'l Cash*."

Shaklin paused. Tilted his head to listen. But the voices of Zheng and Rual were clearer now.

Jump! they were saying. *Jump!*

And so his hand came down toward the panel.

But then Sten's voice said: "We heard you got yourselves in a jam, mates, and we've come a long way to get you out of it."

Shaklin didn't jump.

CHAPTER TWENTY FIVE

FIRST CONTACT

Sten sat hunched over the comboard, knowing that the first words that came out of his mouth would set the tone for what happened next.

Success. Or abject failure.

On the monitor screen, he could see the enhanced image of the *Flame* and the immense space-train in its charge.

The space-train was drawn up in a circle, reminding Sten of pictures he'd seen in old fiches of human pioneers on ancient Earth daring the wilderness in animal-powered wagons.

The *Flame* hovered over its charges, like a fierce mother Gurion guarding her charges. Instead of the starfish-like arms of the Gurion, many-colored connector beams emanated from the sleek ship, linking all the cargo barges and their tugs. In addition, scores of small tender-bots patrolled the train, on the constant lookout for mechanical breakdowns, or damage from meteor hits. Repair and maintenance units scurried over the cargo containers, like swarms of ants tending their nests.

From this perspective, the *Flame* looked like a living being, so large and so complex that it formed its own environment—like the great clonal colonies that forested the planet Aspen in the distant Pando Sector.

The *Flame* and its treasure of raw Imperium X was Sten's goal. His target. His mission. But to think of it that way for too long would be a mistake. True, it was an engineering miracle. He could devote a lifetime studying the history of how such marvels came into being.

Why, the very ship he was on—the *Jo'l Cash*—was the identical twin sister of the *Flame*. Proof of just how successful the engineer creators had been.

But although the *Flame* looked, and sometimes even behaved like a living being, in the end, it was only a thing. To capture the thing—the inanimate object—he had to first capture the minds of the nearly two hundred crew members who formed the true core of the *Flame*

He put aside the ship. Flipped a switch so the image of the *Flame* was replaced by a roster of the crewmembers.

Sten scrolled through the enlistment pictures, pausing here and there to study a face. Wondering how that face—looking so proud and hopeful upon enlistment—became a traitor. A mutineer.

He came to the conclusion that in reality, they really weren't that much different than the sailors who made up the crew of the *Jo'l Cash*.

Never mind the ring leaders. To hell with Shaklin and his bizarre beliefs; or Rual, the enforcer; or Zheng, the toad who thought he was The Big Boss. No, get the Unholy Three out of your mind. Aim your words at the crew, a hard-working grease-stained bunch who'd just as soon be bending their elbows and resting their butts on a stool at the nearest Local.

They'd be scared. Confused. Probably wondering how they got themselves into this mess.

And so he drew in a deep breath, keyed the mike, and said:

"This is Captain Sten, aboard the *Jo'l Cash*.

"We heard you were in trouble, mates, and we've come a long way to help you out."

He gave it a few heartbeats to let the words sink in, then he said: "Right about now, you're all probably worried about your future. I know I would be. And I'd also be wondering what my family and friends were thinking back on my homeworld. Would they think I was a traitor? Are my folks hanging their heads in shame when neighbors pass? And my school chums. I'd be worried about what they were thinking. And what about the guys down at my Local? Are they wondering what the clot happened. What went wrong?"

ABOARD THE *FLAME*

Sten's words echoed through the ship. Shaklin glanced around. Everyone was transfixed. Frozen in place. Even Rual was entirely still. Only Zheng's long, pink tongue nervously flicked out to lick his thick lips.

Captain Sten continued: "I don't know about you guys, but there was this scrote in my group who acted like he was everybody's best friend, but soon as your back was turned, he'd be sniping at you. Putting the blame on you when it was something he'd done. You know the type. And he was always after my girl, you know? Telling stories. Lies about how he saw me with some slut, or other."

Shaklin saw the looks on faces of the sailors. Nodding. Yeah, they all knew a guy like that. Frowning. Yeah, and that guy would be sneaking around their sweetheart right about now. Whispering lies in her ear. Except—well, now it looked like those lies weren't so untruthful after all.

Sten said: "I remember how proud everybody was when I signed on. I worked so clottin' hard studying to pass the merchantman's test. And then I went through all that training. Boot camp and specialist schools. Man, it was tough. Really tough. And boy was I proud when I went home on leave and hugged my mom and shook my dad's hand. He had a tear in his eye, he was so proud. Said it was his allergies acting up again."

Shaklin heard laughter and knew some sailors were remembering their own homecoming, their own fathers wiping away a tear.

And Sten said: "I don't know about you, but I was the first person in my family to make it that far. To go beyond just basic school and get an actual decent-paying job with health and pension benefits. I remember how proud I was at the Local buying a round for my mates. Laughing at that back-stabbing clot who was so jealous he could spit.

"And that night. After hours. What a cuddle I got from my girl. Her eyes shining. Whispering my name. Promising she'd always be there. Waiting for me…"

Shaklin heard Sten pause. Letting the silence work for him. Shaklin knew he was being manipulated. But everything rang so true, he didn't care.

And then Sten continued: "Sure, everything was wonderful back then. I figured I had life licked. Nothing but shining times ahead. Adventures in far off lands.

"And I made so many promises to myself. I'd work hard, by God, and not slough off. I'd climb that promotion ladder. Stash credits in the bank. Someday I'd go home and marry my girl. I'd still be young, and I'd have a pension plus maybe another job because I was a skilled spacer, and me and my family would be living good life, man...the good life."

Shaklin could see people nodding, eyes turned inward, remembering how it was.

And Sten said: "But then something happened. And everything changed. It was horrible. Horrible. Like the Devil Himself was whispering in my ear.

"And I went for it. Don't ask me how. Don't ask me why. I just did it, man. And now I'm fucked. Good and fucked. And I don't know how to get the hell out of this clottin' mess. If I could only turn back the clock."

Shaklin heard Rual curse and saw her start toward the com board, intent on chopping off the deadly words that were undermining everything.

"Here, there!" someone shouted and Rual stopped. Looked around. People were glaring at her. She looked at Zheng, who just shook his head. Better not.

Rual shrugged—as if on second thought she didn't care—and backed away. But Shaklin could tell she was burning inside.

Then he realized that the Sten had stopped speaking.

Shaklin knew damned well that Sten was artfully letting the long silence build suspense.

Even so, he ached for him to continue. To show them all the way out of their dilemma.

CHAPTER TWENTY SIX

TURNING THE SCREW

Aboard the *Jo'l Cash*, Sten looked over at Doc, who had been timing the speech, jotting notes on a knee pad.

A raised eyebrow asked: How're we doing?

Doc waggled a furry paw. So, so.

Sten grimaced. Wringing an opinion from Doc was next to impossible. He waited while Doc did some kind of internal count.

Finally, he signaled: Go!

Sten drew in a breath to steady himself. Time to seal the deal with the mutineers. Or, fall flat on his face.

He keyed the mike and said: "Well, mates, that's why we're here. The Eternal Emperor himself heard about your trouble and sent us to sort things out. You are probably thinking the Emp's just another Big Boss who doesn't give a drakh about poor swabbies like us. Well, that's not the truth, mates. Not the truth at all.

"The Emp personally got on the horn to me and said, 'Captain Sten, I hear some of my sailors on the *Flame* have got themselves in a spot of bother. I've seen their records and they look like a pretty good bunch who just got led astray...'"

ABOARD THE *FLAME*

Shaklin was amazed at the impact Sten's words were having on the crew. Even his own congregants were hanging on every syllable.

He doubted that the Eternal Emperor actually spoke personally to this man. But part of him wanted to believe. Ached to believe.

And Sten said: "The Emp told me—'Here, Captain, I want you to take this ship and get yourself to Possnet Sector. Speak to my people in person. Find out what is truly in their hearts. And tell them, by God, I'll do everything in my power to set things right.'"

There was another long, suspense-building pause, and then Sten said: *"And so I'm here to do just that.* In exactly one E-hour I'm going to come on board and talk to you in person. Also, we have mail for you—from your families. And if you have mail to send out, we'll be happy to take care of that for you."

Suddenly Zheng's emotional dam burst. He grabbed a mike and shouted into it: "Stop! Lies you are telling! Imperial lies! You are not welcome here. I swear, you move one meter, even, and we will jump!"

ABOARD THE *JO'L CASH*

Sten glanced over at Doc, who said, "It's Zheng, the ringleader."

Sten nodded. Keyed the mike. "I hear you, Zheng. No need to get your jock in a twist."

Zheng shouted back: "Respect, I insist on! If speak, you must, speak with respect."

Sten chuckled. "Sure, sure, Zheng. I respectfully hear you. And I'm respectfully asking you not to get your jock in a twist. The *Jo'l Cash* will stay at distance, so there's no need to be nervous. I'll use the ship's lighter. It's not armed, so there's no danger to you."

Zheng was so distraught he practically screamed: "Come alone, you must! Alone!"

Sten said, "Sure, I'll come alone. Alone plus my ace boon coon, Alex Kilgour."

"Not acceptable," Zheng insisted. "One only. Only one must come."

"Not happening," Sten said. "Either both of us come, or I'll turn around and go back to the Emperor and tell him a scrote named Zheng put a kibosh on the whole thing. Meanwhile, you can explain to your mates how come they're all be facing a firing squad because you insisted on playing the 'my way or the slideway' game."

ABOARD THE *FLAME*

Shaklin watched Zheng visibly crumble. At first he was flush with angry self-importance, but when Zheng looked around and saw the other crew members glaring at him and muttering to each other, he his sloped shoulders sagged even more, his pigeon chest seemed to collapse, and his bow legs became even more pronounced.

Just then a red pinlight began flashing on the com board. Shaklin went to answer, but then saw the call was coming in on the freq that Zheng had declared was for his own private use.

Rual spotted it and nudged her boss. Whispered in his ear. Zheng's eyes widened, then keyed into the line.

He turned away so no one could see or hear what he was saying. A minute later he cut the connection and turned back, a huge smile on his toadish face.

He keyed the mike. "Very well, Captain Sten," He said. "You come. Friend come also. Talk you. Listen we."

"Very well," Sten replied. "We'll be with you in exactly one E-hour."

Zheng cut the connection, a look of supreme confidence on his face.

Shaklin didn't have to ask who had called.

It could only have been Queen Venatora.

CHAPTER TWENTY SEVEN

BOARDING THE FLAME

A young crewman met them in the locker and escorted Sten and Alex to the bridge. From his looks and the demeanor of the others, discipline was at rock bottom.

Their uniforms were shabby and unwashed, and they all smelled like they hadn't seen the inside of a fresher for weeks.

When Sten and Alex strode into the room, Zheng came forward to greet them—a glowering Rual at his side. In the background, Sten spotted Shaklin and his congregants gathered around the Holoimager with its dazzling display of the Possnet Sector.

Sten immediately spotted areas where his navigators aboard the *Flame* had surmised that Venatora and her pirate forces were arrayed. In one corner he saw a blinking yellow light he knew was the *Jo'l Cash*.

He'd never seen such detail in a holoimager and had to drag his attention away to deal with the mutineers. Besides, Ida would be monitoring and recording everything on the bridge.

Zheng came stumping up to them on his bow legs, saying, "Captain Sten. Too late almost you were. Handsome new offer we have from Queen Venatora."

Rual made a nasty noise Sten could only assume was laughter.

"Handsome is right," she said. "Enough to make us all clottin' millionaires. We were about to vote on it when you showed up."

Next to him, Alex seemingly caught his toe on the edge of a gravchair and stumbled. He recovered, muttering a curse at his own clumsiness.

Sten had to suppress a smile. Kilgour had just planted the first of many bugs he planned to scatter about the ship during their visit. They were the latest from the Mantis Section's snooping arsenal and were virtually undetectable.

Rual smirked. "A little nervous?" she said.

Kilgour just shrugged, using the gesture to scatter a few more bugs.

Turning to Zheng, Rual added, "Probably had a couple of pops to work up his courage."

This drew a laugh from Zheng. But before he could make a mocking observation of his own, Sten stepped past them, as if they weren't there.

"What about it, shipmates?" he said to the assembled crew. "Were you really going to vote before you heard what your Commander in Chief had to say about the deplorable conditions aboard this ship?"

He reached into his breast pocket and slowly, very deliberately, drew out an official looking document and held it up before the crew.

"What I have here," he said, "is the official announcement of—"

Rual tried to snatch the document away, but Kilgour easily blocked her.

"Here, now," he said. "Captain Sten has the floor. "Every swingin' scrote of ye will gie yer turn when the time's proper."

Rual fumbled for her knife, but Kilgour clamped his big hand around her wrist and gave it a squeeze. Rual gasped and the knife clattered to the floor.

Zheng was so furious he was practically spitting his words. "Gutt damn! How dare you!" He slapped his chest. "Here...on the *Flame*...I command."

He waved a hand, taking in the entire bridge. "I command all. One word..." He held up a single finger, which shook with rage. "One word. One word only. And we space you."

Sten chuckled. "Lieutenant Kilgour," he said. "The man's an even bigger fool than Personnel made him out to be."

Alex shook his head, looking mournful. "Sich a pity," he said. "It's his poor mither, I feel sorry for."

As he spoke, he slipped another bug into a likely spot.

Sten turned back to Zheng. "Did you really think we came aboard without any support or backup?"

Zheng frowned. "Vhatt do you mean? Vhatt support. Vhatt backup? I see nothing."

Sten chuckled. "You know that lighter that's tied up to your ship? That nice little rig nobody bothered to check out before we came aboard?"

Zheng shot Rual a questioning look. She grimaced. "Gutt damn!" Zheng muttered. "Gutt damn!"

Sten laughed. "You guessed it," he said. "One wrong move, and..." He threw his hands apart in a mock explosion."

"Big clottin' deal," Rual said. "You'll die, too." She turned to the crew. "He's bluffing," she said. "That's all it is. A big clottin' bluff."

Instead of replying, Sten turned back to the crew. "What about it, shipmates?" he said. "Do you want to hear me out? Or lay hands on us and see if we're bluffing?"

A murmur swept the group. Finally, Shaklin came forward.

"We'll hear you out, Captain," he said. "But you'd better make it good. Zheng wasn't lying when he said Venatora made us a handsome offer."

"Obviously, the Emperor can beat any monetary offer she made," Sten said. "I'm authorized to top any amount by twenty percent."

Another murmur swept the group. There were smiles at first. But then cold reality sank in.

"What about amnesty?" Shaklin said. "For some of us, that's more important than the money."

"Don't you be saying what's more important, Holy Man," Rual broke in.

Shaklin turned to the others. "What about it? Am I right? Isn't amnesty the most important thing?"

Everyone quickly agreed that it was.

"In that case," Sten said, "take a look at this."

He held up the document. "You're Bishop Shaklin, right?"

Shaklin nodded, took the document and opened it. As he scanned it several of his congregants and a couple of the crew-members came forward to peer over his shoulder.

Then they all looked up Sten, gaping in surprise.

"Why, this...this...this is a Court Martial filing," Shaklin said.

"Vhatt's that?" Zheng cried. "Court martial? I vill not be court martialed!"

Sten laughed. "Among your many problems, Zheng," he said,

"is that you suffer from delusions of reference. Big time."

Zheng sputtered. "Delusions? Delusions? Vhatt's this delusions?"

"He means that this is for Gregor, Zheng," Shaklin said, "not you."

Zheng and Rual looked at Shaklin, then Sten and Alex. Flabbergasted.

Sten said, "One of my jobs today is to open proceedings for the court martial of Captain Gregor Wichman."

The mutineers gaped at Sten. Of all things, no one ever dreamed Gregor would face a court martial board.

Shaklin was the first to recover. "Open proceedings?" he said. "What does that mean exactly?"

"It means that Lt. Kilgour and I are to take statements from you and others members of the crew. We have already gathered extensive evidence of Captain Gregor's illegal dealings at Port Chinen and other areas on the *Flame*'s shipping route. Which is the main reason for our delay in getting to you."

Sten let his gaze sweep across the group, then added, "When we're done here, I will immediately return to my ship and report my findings directly to the Eternal Emperor."

Zheng shook his head. "Nonsense, this is," he said. "No, not nonsense but a trick. You will tie us up here with the gutt damned red tape and then—"

Shaklin interrupted. "What about that, Captain?" he said. "Zheng makes a good point. We all know about Imperial red tape. We've all been victims of it one time or another."

There were mutters of agreement from the other members of the crew. Rual started to interrupt, but Zheng gave her the elbow.

"Yes, Captain?" he said. "Vhatt do you have to say about that?"

"I'm dealing directly with the Eternal Emperor," Sten said. "So there will be no red tape. I'll have a decision for you within 24 E-hours."

"And if you don't?" Shaklin pressed.

Sten shrugged. "Then, obviously, you'll take Venatora's offer and the Emperor will be out of luck."

"We'll want guarantees," Shaklin said.

"And you'll have them," Sten said.

"I don't like it," Zheng said.

"You got that right," Rual chimed in.

"What do you have to lose?" Sten said. "Either I deliver, or I don't."

There was great deal of back and forth argument, with Zheng and Rual pushing for refusal.

But Sten had undercut their authority so much that, in the end, it was agreed. Sten and Alex could move through the ship and interview the crew, gathering evidence again Gregor.

While they argued, Shaklin took them aside. "You'll have to move fast," he said. "Two hours at the most. Otherwise they'll be at your throats."

"Two hours it is, then," Sten said. "But to speed things up, I want to talk to Gregor first."

"He'll just lie," Shaklin said.

"That just makes it better for your cause, Bishop," Sten said. "Because he'll be lying under oath. That's perjury. And in this case..."

He paused, giving Shaklin a look of great empathy. "I understand there was more than one death involved in Gregor's activities," he said.

Tears welled in Shaklin's eyes. He nodded. "Yes..." his voice almost broke. He steeled himself. "At least one," he said.

"Her name?" Sten asked.

"You obviously know about it," Shaklin said.

Sten nodded. "Pegatha, right?" he said. "Your friend."

"Yes. She was my...friend," Shaklin said. "Her death was listed as an accident. But Gregor might as well have killed her himself."

"If that's the case," Sten said, "he may very well face a firing squad."

Shaklin knuckled an eye. "Come on," he said. "I'll take you to him."

As the navigator led them down the passageway, it gave Sten no joy to think what an accomplished liar he had become.

CHAPTER TWENTY EIGHT

GREGOR'S DILEMMA

Gregor braced himself when he heard the footsteps approach the cabin door. The mutineers had kept him deaf and blind in this little room. But his guards had been so keyed up the past few hours he knew that something was about to break.

When the door whooshed open he was half expecting to see whoever the Emperor had sent to negotiate with his captors, and he had all his best lies at the ready.

He saw Shaklin first, which was a surprise. He'd expected Zheng or Rual. And then he saw a squat, tubby man with a round bearded face. He wore lieutenant bars on the shoulders of his Imperial Navy uniform.

A lieutenant? He couldn't imagine that the Emperor had sent a mere lieutenant to negotiate the release of such a valuable cargo.

Then he saw the third man. He was a little taller than the lieutenant, but not by much. He was built like gymnast, and he was dark, with sharp features and fiery eyes. It was a familiar face, but it wasn't until he saw the sardonic half-grin and heard the voice that full recognition dawned.

"Hello, Gregor," the man said.

"You!" he said. "Sten!"

"In the flesh," Sten said.

Gregor stabbed a finger at the captain's bars on Sten's shoulders.

"How...how..." he gobbled. Then envy overtook him. This was so unfair.

"But, you...you...you...were a nobody," he said.

"And you thought you were a somebody," Sten said. "And look where it got you."

Shaklin was puzzled. "You know each other?" he asked.

"We were in basic training together," Sten said. "He was always bragging about what an important person his father was."

"Ah ken the bugger washed out," Alex said.

"You heard right," Sten said.

Shaklin looked at Sten, sudden doubt in his eyes. "He said you were a nobody. Surely, the Emperor didn't send someone of low importance to negotiate with us."

"He didn't," Sten said. "If you look at my credentials again you'll see that my uncle is Admiral Mik Ledoh. Until recently I was his flag lieutenant."

Gregor snorted derision. "Liar!" he said. "You acted like you were just one of the guys. And here you were lying to us the whole time and had a clotting admiral to back your act. Why, you were a made man the minute you joined up. No wonder Lanzotta was always singing your praises."

Sten turned to Shaklin. "You don't want to hear any of this garbage," he said. "Besides, for the purposes of this court martial report, we have to interview the suspect in private."

"Court martial?" Gregor cried. "Suspect?"

Kilgour reached over and swatted the back of his head. It appeared to be just a light tap, but Gregor nearly fell off his bunk.

"Shut it," Kilgour explained.

Gregor shut it. Shaklin couldn't help the huge grin that spread across his face.

"Call me when you're ready," he said.

And he exited, confident that he was leaving Gregor in hostile hands. Within minutes every being aboard the ship had a good chuckle when they heard about the slap.

When he was gone, Gregor said, "They're not really going to court martial me are then?" Rubbing the back of his head, he added, "I mean, I'm the victim here."

"First off," Sten said, "you still have a big clotting mouth, and if you want to get out this in one piece you'll start shutting it."

Gregor nodded. "Okay," he said. "Sorry."

"Second," Sten said, "You ought to know that any captain who loses his ship for any reason must face a court martial."

"But—" Gregor started to protest.

Alex raised a meaty hand, and the protest died a quick death.

"Naturally, with your old man being such a hot shot," Sten

said, "you'll not only get off, but you'll probably end up with a medal."

Gregor nodded vigorously. "Gotcha," he said. "It's all an act."

"We have express orders to bring you home alive and well," Sten said. "So get that worry out of your head and start cooperating."

"Done and done," Gregor said.

Sten fished a small box out of his pocket. He opened it, revealing an even smaller box nestled in soft material.

"This is a special com unit," Sten said, "courtesy of your old man. It's a direct link to him. And he wants to talk to you privately—and I stress privately—at your first opportunity."

Gregor took it.

"An don't be rattlin' oan to yer Da'loch a lass pratlin' to 'er mates," Alex warned. "Or yoo'll tip yer hand to Mr. Toad Face and his boyos."

"Okay, I got all that," Gregor said. "But what's your plan for getting me the clot out of here?"

His confidence was returning now that he knew that his influential father was close. He tilted his head, and Sten recognized that look of arrogance that used to drive him and the rest of the barracks mad.

Although Kilgour hadn't been around then, he must have caught it too, because his hand shot out and—*whap!*—he swatted the back of Gregor's head.

This time Gregor fell to the floor. "Hey!" he cried. "What was that for?"

"Ye hae the look ay th' son of a huir abit ye, laddie," Kilgour said. "That's what's for."

Gregor started to protest, then thought better of it.

"Sorry," he said, not meaning a syllable of it, and climbed back onto his bunk.

"Now that we have that settled," Sten said, "here's what is going to happen. When we leave here, we'll signal your father and he'll get in touch with you. I understand he has specific instructions."

"Uh, can I ask—" he stopped, glancing at Kilgour to see if he'd broken some rule. Alex nodded, and so he continued. "Quick question. Will you be able to listen in when I speak to my father."

"Of course, not," Sten lied. "Your father requested complete privacy, and our techs made sure that you have it."

Out of the corner of his eye he saw Alex plant a couple more bugs just to make sure that nothing Gregor said or did would be missed.

"Now, when we get back to our ship we'll get further instructions from the brass," Sten said. "Then we'll continue our negotiations. If they agree, we have ships standing by to take control of the space-train, and you'll soon be in a nice comfortable cabin and on your way home."

"And if they don't agree?" Gregor sounded worried.

Sten shrugged. "It'll take a little longer to get the upper hand, is all," he said. "In the end it will work out the same."

"Okay, then," Gregor said. "I'll be waiting to hear from my father. And then from you."

"That's the spirit," Sten said and he turned to rap on the door.

"Wait a minute," Gregor said.

Sten paused, giving him a quizzical look. "Yes?"

"Did you guys, uh, bring me anything to eat?"

Kilgour muttered a curse and almost hit him again, but Gregor jumped back out of range.

"They've been feeding me nothing but drakh," he whined. "I'm clotting dying in here from food poisoning."

"I'll speak to them," Sten said, and then he rapped on the door.

It was another lie, which delighted Sten to no end when he thought about the good laugh his old barracksmates would have if they had witnessed Gregor getting well-deserved paybacks.

CHAPTER TWENTY NINE

THE NEGOTIATIONS

A few hours later, Sten and Alex finished interviewing a dozen crewmembers, hearing one tale of woe after another.

And Gregor was at the black-hearted core of every tale.

They ranged from the petty—one crew member had, in his words, "cut a stinky pratt" in the control room in Gregor's presence and got a month in the brig for his offense—to the more serious: another crew member was forced to hand over her pay directly to Gregor for a solid year for queering a black market deal—to outright cruelty: a crewmember who wasn't moving fast enough during an exercise lost her eyesight when Gregor failed to close a valve controlling a fluorine feed on time. Everyone believed the act was deliberate.

Sten, who had lost his family in an incident involving fluorine, was particularly angered by the last.

The final person they interviewed was Shaklin, who told them every damning detail about the death of his lover, Pegatha, brought about by Gregor's malfeasance.

They sat in his cabin while he told the tale as manfully as possible, eyes brimming, voice shaking, beaded dreadlocks atremble, but he never shed a tear. And when he was done the three sat in silence for long minutes.

Finally, Shaklin asked: "Tell me the truth. Will he really face a court martial?"

"He will," Sten said, hoping this would not turn out to be a lie.

"But, what about his father?" Shaklin pressed. "He's an important man. A rich man. With rich and powerful friends. Gregor says his father is tight with the Emperor."

Sten made a derisive noise. He said, "The Emperor would like nothing more than to see Gregor and his old man skinned alive.

This whole thing has been an incredible embarrassment to him, and he wants it shut down as quickly as possible before the embarrassment becomes public knowledge."

Shaklin sighed. "That's sounds too good to be true," he said. "In my whole life I've never known real justice."

"Well, this time you are going to get it," Sten said. He paused, then added, "But we'll need your help to bring it off."

Shaklin's eyebrows rose. "Help?"

Sten said, "Zheng and Rual appear as mentally stable as a pair of Xypacas on a starvation diet."

"That's no understatement," Shaklin said.

"With them running things," Sten said, "a sneeze could send this whole enterprise off the rails. If that happens, the Emperor will send Mantis teams to track down you, your people, and everyone else aboard the *Flame*. No one will ever see the inside of a courtroom. Clot, they won't even find themselves in marked graves. We're talking cut throats all around and bodies shunted into space."

Shaklin shuddered. "I've heard of things like that," he said. "But I thought they were just tales."

"They're not tales," Sten said. "The point is, the last thing you want is to get yourself on the Eternal Emperor's enemies list. Someone once told me that if someone really drakhs him off, he'll set aside five minutes every day to think about that shitepoke until he seals his fate."

"In other words, lad," Kilgour said, "if it's justice yer wantin' for wee Pegatha, yer gonna hae to help us."

Shaklin took a deep breath. Then nodded.

"How?" he asked.

Sten produced a small clear plas box and handed it over. "Here's a com unit," he said. "A direct link to us. It's shielded from all other com units on the ship, so it can't be interfered with by outside sources."

Shaklin tucked the box away.

Sten said, "If things look like they are going to go sideways, give us shout. And we'll do the same for you."

"Got it," Shaklin said.

Sten added, "The main thing is, you have to keep Gregor safe long enough for us to get our hands on him. Without Gregor, there can be no court martial. And without a court martial, there will be no justice because the blame will fall squarely on you and your shipmates."

Alex put a sympathetic hand on his shoulder. "'Tis th' onliest way ye'll get yer revenge, laddie," he said. "And th' onliest way you and yer mates'll be safe."

Shaklin wiped moisture from his eyes, made a grim smile, then he led them back to the control room where Zheng and the others waited.

CHAPTER THIRTY

THE OFFER

The atmosphere crackled with tension. The crewmembers were gathered in small muttering groups. Zheng was sprawled in a gravchair, toadish face flushed with drink. Rual stood behind the chair, toying with her long knife.

They all looked up when Sten, Alex and Shaklin entered.

"Took your clottin' time," Rual snarled, waving the knife about.

"Patient long enough, ve haf been," Zheng said, swinging around to plant his feet on the floor.

He started to rise, thought better of it, and sank woozily back into his seat.

"And a protest, I must make," he continued. "Everyone you speak to about Gregor—except us." He indicated Rual and himself. "Complaints we have as well. A criminal, that man is."

"We have more than enough for a proper court martial without your input," Sten said.

"Still. Insist, I must," Zheng said.

"Yeah," Rual put in. "We clottin' insist."

"Insist all you like," Sten said. "But I'm afraid any testimony you two gave would do more harm to your cause than good."

"Harm? Vat is this harm, you speak of?" demanded Zheng.

"Both of you have extensive criminal records," Sten said. "Kidnapping. Fraud. Theft. Violence. Possible murders, even."

There were gasps of surprise from the crewmembers. Obviously, Zheng and Rual had kept them in the dark about their backgrounds."

"What's this, Zheng?" someone shouted. "You didn't tell us you had a record."

There were other shouts and protests. Zheng struggled to his feet and turned on them.

"Lies," he cried. "All lies." He pointed at Sten. "He vants to turn you against us. Discord, he vants to sow."

Rual waved her knife at the group. "Watch yer tongues," she said. "Or, I'll cut them out."

Sten raised a hand. "Shipmates!" he called out. "Calm yourselves. We're here to talk about more important things than who is a criminal and who is not."

There were a few more angry retorts, but gradually everyone calmed down—except for Rual, who was so agitated Sten wondered if maybe they'd all get lucky and a blood vessel would burst in her teeny brain.

"Remember my purpose," Sten said. "I'm here to make an offer for the return of the Emperor's goods."

That got him the silence he needed.

"First off, I'm going to start with the issue of amnesty. I'm sure that is uppermost in your minds."

"Money, that's all I clotting care about," Rual said. "The rest is drakh."

But from the comments of the crewmembers, her view was far from universally shared.

"From the facts Lt. Kilgour and I have gathered," Sten said, "we have more than enough evidence for a court martial to return a guilty verdict against Captain Gregor."

The reaction from the crew was loud and decidedly positive. Except for Zheng and Rual. The looks they exchanged were murderous to the extreme.

"In fact," Sten went on, "there are several charges that are firing squad offenses."

The roar of approval shook the control room. Crewmembers were embracing and pounding one another on the back.

Only Zheng and Rual looked unhappy. Sten was wondering when one of them might act on their displeasure when he saw Rual tip the nod to two beefy mutineers. They were definitely knuckle draggers of the inbred human variety, with beetled brows, fist-scarred faces and eyes so close together you could put them out with one finger.

Without warning, the two men charged. They were swinging heavy, two-foot long wrenches, and the other crewmembers scrambled out of the way as the thugs closed in on Sten and Alex.

Sten easily slipped the blow of the first man, stepping aside to let him stumble past. He grabbed the thug's wrist as he went, twisting and half-dropping to one knee.

There was an audible *crack!* and a howl of pain as the man's wrist snapped and he flopped to the floor, groaning and cradling his wrist.

"You broke it," he blubbered like a wronged schoolboy.

Meanwhile, Alex didn't bother dodging the blow that was aimed at him. Instead, he caught the heavy wrench in midswing and plucked it away as if from a child. The force of the swing carried the big man forward.

The heavy worlder grabbed him by the elbow, spun him around, and booted him in the arse—lifting him from the deck and sending him flying at Rual.

The thug crashed headfirst at Rual's feet, where he remained, groaning in pain.

Rual peered down at the man, clearly disgusted. She spat on him, then looked up at Sten, eyes burning with hatred.

The command room was dead silent. Everyone stared at Sten and Alex, wondering what was going to happen next.

Sten brushed his hands together, as if ridding them of dirt.

"Now, let's talk money," Sten said, as if nothing untoward had occurred.

Tension immediately drained away, and the crew looked at him expectantly.

Sten named a figure.

The reaction was such that he knew he'd topped whatever Venatora had offered by a wide margin.

He waited until the uproar died down, then said, "Lt. Kilgour and I will return to our ship and let you discuss the terms without interference. If you have any questions before you take your final vote, you only have to call."

With that, he turned and motioned for Shaklin to lead them back to their lighter. At the door, he paused long enough to add, "Just make sure you don't take too long to decide."

Zheng spoke up. "And if more time, we need, what then?" The little toad would be defiant to the last.

"Yeah," Rual said. "What about it?"

Sten stared at both Rual and Zheng long and hard. He said,

"Don't test me. You won't like how it turns out."

Then he was gone, and Zheng was bitterly cursing his name.

The man on the floor tried to sit up. Rual kicked him in the ribs.

CHAPTER THIRTY ONE

THREE HOLY KILGOURS

Ida had a split screen up on the vidwall. On the left, she could see Sten and Alex strapping themselves into the seats of their lighter and going through their flight check list before setting off to the *Jo'l Cash*.

On the right—thanks to the bugs Kilgour had planted—she could monitor the *Flame*'s command room, where crewmembers were gathered around Zheng and Rual. She didn't know what they were saying—for some reason, the sound wasn't working yet—but there was much hand waving, shout-contorted faces, and other signs that Zheng and Rual were resisting demands for an immediate vote to accept the Emperor's offer. But from all appearances they were in the minority. She doubted the ringleaders of the mutiny could resist much longer.

Good. The sooner they got this crazy-ass mission behind them, the sooner she could continue her interrupted vacation. She was anxious to get back to playing the galactic commodities market with her new boy toy. If they put their heads together—as well as other interesting body parts—they could clean up shorting the Imperium X market.

She had a little chuckle over that train of thought. You are getting to be a dirty old Rom woman in your old age, Ida, she thought.

She looked over her shoulder at Doc, who was studying the faces and body movements of the crew, paying particular attention to Zheng and Rual. He'd been oddly quiet for the past hour, and Ida wondered what the furry little vampire was thinking.

"That seemed to go well enough," she said. "Sten and Kilgour kept them off guard the whole time. Sten played the big brother, or the uncle near your age, to a perfect 'T'. Those scrotes were eating it up."

She glanced at the screens, then back at Doc. "Except for Zheng and Rual," she added. "They weren't buying any of it."

Doc scratched his furry ear, and she frowned. This was Doc's *tell*. A natural Doubting Thomas, Doc's psy antenna was almost visibly a-quiver when the doubts went to something worse. When that happened, he got an itch behind his right ear that demanded immediate relief.

"She isn't done escalating yet," he said, indicating Rual. "She's too worked up and can't come down. Somebody needs to hit her with either a triple strength opioid or a padded club, whichever is closest to hand." More ear scratching. "And that clotting Zheng," Doc said. "He's acting like somebody used the above-mentioned padded club on him. It's like he's in a trance, letting Rual rail on without stepping in before she loses control."

Aboard the lighter, Sten and Alex exchanged worried looks. He keyed the mic. "That was my reading, too, Doc," he said. "But now I'm beginning to wonder if it's deliberate. That maybe he wants Rual to blow."

He fished a com unit out of his pocket. "Let me see if I can connect with Shaklin. Get him to step in."

Sten spoke into it. Shook his head. Fiddled with controls, then sighed. "No go. Some kind of interference."

"I'm sorting out the sound, so don't worry," Ida said, sounding a little testy. As if everybody thought the problem was her fault.

"Sure, sure, no problem" Sten said as soothingly as he could. Ida could get touchy when things technical dared to defy her.

"Also, Sten," Ida said, "don't forget you have the garbage option. If things go south, hit that eject button, and fast."

She was reminding him of the Paku Defender she'd stashed in the trash chute. It was basically a shield, but with the nasty habit—from the attackers point of view—of not just warding off explosives, but projecting them back at two or three times the original force.

Sten laughed. "That's right, all I gotta do is take out the trash," he said.

* * * *

Meanwhile, in the *Flame*'s command room, Shaklin was stepping into the fray. Tall and dark, he gave off the auroa of infinite wisdom. In the chaos that had descended upon the command room he was an imposing figure who immediately caught everyone's attention.

Kilgour noted that although the sound was still cut off and he couldn't hear what Shaklin was saying, he had an obvious calming influence on the group. Even Rual seemed to settle down a bit.

Alex drew everyone's attention to the scene. "Dinnae fash, lads and lassies," he said. "Ah have infinit't faith in our wee bishop. He's got th' God of Many Names on his side."

Sten shot Alex a scoffing, give-me-a-break look. "Since when did you get religion, Kilgour?" he said.

Alex looked miffed. "Why, it's a well known fact that all Kilgours are religious," he said. "And we have any number of holy lads and lassies to speak'it to th' Big Man fer us."

"Ri-i-ight," Sten scoffed. He'd heard Alex's views on religion many times and knew his friend to be a staunch atheist like himself.

"Och, ye ay wee faith," Alex said, "it's a weelk-knoon fact 'at aw Kilgours ur religious. Ain we hae onie number ay holy lads and lassies tae speak'it tae th' Big Cheil for us."

"If you say so," Sten said, as he gently separated the lighter from its berth and started away from the *Flame*.

Kilgour put a big hand on his chest as if insulted. "Ye be temptin' the devil, lad," he said. "Ye shoods ken thaur ur Kilgour priests, ministers, rabbis...ye name't it, whatever th' religion there's a Kilgour to uphauld it."

Despite himself, Sten was drawn in. "No wonder there are so many atheists," he said. "Mystery solved. The Kilgour clan is singlehandedly driving people away from religion."

"Nothin' further frae th' truth," Alex protested. "Why, three ay mah great-great uncles waur such miracle workers when it cam tae convertin' th' unfaithful 'at they e'en converted a forest full ay bears."

"Okay, okay," Sten said, stricken with the sudden fear that he had just stepped into a Kilgour shaggy dog story trap. "Never mind that. Pay attention to the com board. We have people who'd like to see us dead, you know."

"Yoo won't gie off sae easily, young Sten," Alex said. "Yoo-have insulted th' dignity of the Shaolin Kilgour!"

A swarm of the *Flame*'s repair bots appeared on the port screen and Sten was kept too busy avoiding them to stop Kilgour's flow.

"One day three of mah uncles waur takin' their ease in a pub," Kilgour said, "discussin't their favorite ways ay convertin' folks.

"They were diff'rint because one uncle was a Catholic priest in good standing, anither was a Baptist minister and th' third was a wee rabbi of the Jewish faith.

"An' although they wair holy men, they fell intae argument abit who was th' best. Fer a real challenge of their convertin' skills, they agreed, wood be tae preach to a bear.

"Weel, one body hin' led tae anither, an they decided on a experiment. They'd each go to th' woods, fin' a bear, preach tae it, an attempt tae convert it tae their religion."

Ida's voice broke in. "Okay, Kilgour, knock it the clot off. This is neither the time or the place for—"

Kilgour cut her off. "Ye got yer nethers in an uproar, lass," he said. "Ah fear religion is th' only cure fur ye."

And with that, he went on:

"So, back to me three uncles. Seven days later they came together to discuss their experiences.

"Father Kilgour—the priest—hud his arm in a sling, was on crutches an' hud bandages aw ower his body. He said, 'I went intae th' wood tae fin' me a bear and when Ah found heem, Ah began to read tae heem frae th' holdy Catechism.

"'Weel, at furst th' bear wanted nae tae do wi' me and began to slap me around. Sae, Ah quickly grabbed me holy water an' sprinkled heem all over his furry body. An'—just like tha'—he became as gentle as a sweet lamb… Th' bishop is comin' next week tae gie heem First Communion an' Confirmation!'"

At that moment the sound aboard the *Flame* cut in and they heard a blood-freezing shriek.

CHAPTER THIRTY TWO

THE ATTACK

That the shriek came from Rual was no surprise.

"Can't you see that Sten's makin' clottin' fools of us," Rual was shouting. "All that sweet talk about court martials and amnesty and enough credits to choke an equine."

"Now, Rual," Shaklin was saying, "there's no reason to get upset. This is just a discussion preliminary to a vote."

"Vote! Vote!" Rual shrieked. "Who said this was a clottin' democracy? Sten's a fraud, I tell you. I'll bet he got a clottin' Imperial battleship standing by. Ready to board us the moment we give in."

Sten and Alex looked at each other. Sten shrugged. That was pretty much the plan.

"And I tell you, they are gonna haul every single man Jack and Jill among us before firing squad," Rual said.

"Come, now," Shaklin said, almost pleading. "Captain Sten had every appearance of being an honorable man. He gave us his word!"

"Word? *Word*?" Rual thundered. "I'll show you what I think of his clottin' word! Drakh, that's all it is! Drakh!"

And with that, she lunged toward the weapons' board.

Sten heard Ida shout, "Eject! Eject!"

And his hand was going for the Paku Defender trigger just as Rual hit the switch.

* * * *

Aboard the *Jo'l Cash*, Ida and Doc saw everyone diving on Rual, but it was too late. The missile had been launched. At this point, the lighter was only about six klicks from the *Flame* and the explosion was almost instantaneous.

Ida switched to another view and saw the immediate aftereffect. A blinding white flash enveloped the little ship. But a moment later the lighter emerged from the flash, unscathed and shot away at a blinding speed.

At the same time, the explosion rippled backward, hitting the *Flame*.

Another explosion. This time engulfing the tail section of the mutineers' ship.

It glowed an eerie golden color, then the color faded and tail section emerged seemingly undamaged, except for a black charring streak where the name of the ship had been painted.

Ida got the bugs aboard the *Flame* operational again and saw that Shaklin and several members of his congregation had Rual pinned up against the wall.

But instead of being furious, Rual was laughing.

"Now, that's torn it," she was shouting. "Whether any of you like it or not, we just gave Sten his answer."

Her words so stunned the group that they let her shake loose.

"The only choice we've got," she said, "is to hit him now and hit him as hard as we can. Then jump the clot out of this sector before Sten has a chance to hit back."

Zheng shook off the stupor he'd sunk into. "Rual, sometimes crazy, she is," he said. "But stupid she is not.

"She is right. Hit him, we must. Every missile we must fire. And then jump. Far, far away we must jump."

"Someplace the Emperor can never find us," Rual said. "And then we can contact Venatora again. Sell the stuff and go about our merry richman's way!"

Zheng moved toward the weapon board. At the same time— aboard the *Jo'l Cash*—Ida's hands were moving toward her own bank of weapons.

She'd obliterate the wench. Unfortunately, she'd be wiping out the Imperium X train at the same time. And that was definitely not in their mission orders.

Aboard the lighter, Sten saw a strange wavering motion just to the left of the Holoimager.

Guessing what Ida was about to do, he jumped in.

"Ida, wait!"

Ida said, "Are you crazy, if I wait we'll all be burnt toast."

"Just wait," Sten ordered.

Cursing under her breath, Ida waited.

And then the wavering image aboard the *Flame* firmed. Until it became that of a remarkably beautiful woman.

It was Venatora.

And at that moment all the bugs aboard the *Flame* went dark.

* * * *

In the control room of the *Jo'l Cash*, Ida stared at the blank screen.

"Drakh," she said. "And fall back in it."

CHAPTER THIRTY THREE

GREGOR'S REVENGE

Sten fished out his com unit, flipped it to Shaklin's mode, then spoke into it:

"Shaklin? This is Sten. If you hear me, don't try to speak unless no one is around. Click once for 'yes,' twice for 'no'" He paused, then, "Do you read me?"

After an agonizing wait there came a single click—yes.

"Are we in any immediate danger?"

There was double click—no.

"They aren't going to fire on us again?"

Double click—no.

In background Ida started chattering. "You don't know if we can trust him, Sten. I vote we don't take any unnecessary changes with these clots."

Sten waved for her to shut up. She did.

He spoke into the mike: "Venatora's there, right?"

A bit of a wait. Shaklin was probably surprised that he knew. Then came a single click—yes.

"Okay, look, I still think we can work this out with as little bloodshed as possible. Everybody will still get their amnesty and they'll still get the credits the Emperor promised. So the question now, is—are you still with me?"

Instead of one click, or two, there were a series of clicks. Click-clickclickclickclick. Then a pause.

"What th' clot goin' on with the wee bairn?" Kilgour said.

Sten finally got it. He said, "And Gregor, Shaklin. The same deal with Gregor. He gets court martialed to the high heavens... So, are you with me?"

There came an immediate single click—yes!

"Excellent," Sten said. "Just stand by and monitor what's going on. Then, soon as you can get to a safe place where we talk, give me a call. Got that?"

A single click—yes.

And then the connection was broken.

ABOARD THE *FLAME*

Gregor blinked like a mole as he was hustled out of his dimly-lit cabin into the bright passageway.

His limbs were stiff from days of inactivity, and he stumbled and nearly fell, only to be brought up short by the two burly crewmen who were his escorts.

"Clumsy scrote," one of the sailors hissed. "Keep yer feet under yers while yer still got legs to walk with."

"I hear Rual's gonna start by breakin' both his knees," the other sailor said.

The first sailor laughed, then gave Gregor a clout alongside the head.

"What he needs is a good Tahn six pack," he said. He made his hand into a pistol. "Two rounds in the ankle. Two in the knees. And two in the elbows."

"A Tahn six-pack... I like that," the second man said.

Gregor kept his mouth shut and hobbled along. He wasn't worried in the least. For the first time since he was overwhelmed in his cabin when the mutiny broke out, he felt like he was finally back in charge.

Well, not exactly in charge. But well on his way to same.

He'd contacted his father with the device Sten had given him, and the old man laid out his whole plan. It was frightening at first—Gregor's life would never be the same again. But it soon became obvious that Lord Wichman not only had everything well under control, but had once again proven himself to be the King of the Deal Makers.

"You just hang on, son," he told Gregor, "and when this is over we'll have so much power even the Eternal Emperor himself will fear us."

Gregor kept those words close as the guards hustled him along, and then a moment later he was shoved into Control Room with such force that he sprawled on his face in front of the assembled crew.

There were cheers and jeers and someone kicked him in the ribs. But after much rough treatment during his captivity, he was prepared for it and doubled up just as the boot connected, lessening the force of the blow.

Then he heard a woman's imperious voice bark a command: "Let him up! We can't talk business with his father if he finds his son face-down on the deck."

Someone pulled him roughly to his feet. Gregor looked around, fighting to keep a smile from spreading across his face.

There was Zheng, with his fat toad face. And Rual, who looked crazier than ever, with her hair standing on end and her eyes on fire. And then there was Shaklin who looked on him with such icy hatred that it froze Gregor to the marrow.

Someone helped him to his feet in a less than gentle manner, and he found himself looking upon the most beautiful woman he had ever seen in his life.

It was Venatora—not in the flesh, but in a live holocast—looking every centimeter the pirate queen.

Gregor tried to speak, but her presence was such that all he could manage was stuttered, "M-my…Lady!"

The crew burst out laughing at this, and there was more jeering and several sailors made squeaky-voiced imitations of his "M-my…Lady!"

Gregor coughed, then tried again, fighting for the confidence his father had tried to instill in him.

"Yes, I have, My Lady," he said. "My father filled in me on the details of the agreement that you and he have hammered out."

"Excellent," Venatora said. "I have already told the others about the plan, but they rightly demanded that I offer proof of the agreement."

"I can help with that, My Lady," Gregor said.

He fumbled in his pocket, but one of his guards swatted him, growling, "Here, none of that sneaky drakh Captain. What'cha got in there?"

Zheng broke in, commanding: "Leave him be, Guttdammit!"

Chastened, the guard stepped away. Gregor hastily fished out the little com unit Sten had given him and placed it on a nearby table.

The Control Center fell silent as everyone in the room stared at the little black box.

Venatora prodded Gregor into action. "Go on," she said.

And Gregor pressed down on the little box and backed away. It made a beeping sound and started to glow. Gradually, a form began to take shape.

* * * *

Across the room, Shaklin huddled with his congregants, furious at what he had just heard from Venatora's lovely lips. He and the others had been betrayed, betrayed.

And the architect of that betrayal rose up from that little box until, standing in front of them—in a live holocast straight from Prime World—was Gregor's father, Lord Wichman.

He of the huge pile of hay-colored hair. He of the round, fleshy face and cold, boring eyes that had never known defiance. He of the loud, hail-fellow tones that were always on the make.

And as Shaklin looked on, that big voice boomed out, "Greetings, Lady Venatora. Good to be with you again."

The image wavered a little as Wichman turned his big body, clad in a stylish businessman's suit. He looked out over the awed crewmembers.

"I bring tremendous news for all of you," he said. "What you are about to hear from me is huge. Huge! You think you know what rich is, well, let me tell you my friends, as a man who is richer than just about anybody in the Empire—except a few other guys, and of course that big crook, the Eternal Emperor—that you are about to be richer than you could have ever dreamed."

He paused, flashed an enormous grin at Zheng and Rual.

"And you owe it all to Queen Venatora and your wise leaders, Zheng and Rual..."

Shaklin looked over at Gregor, who wore a smile that was the twin of his father's.

He began to tremble. One of his people—Murgas, he thought it was—sensed his distress and touched his shoulder, whispering, "Easy, Bishop. Easy. Nothing we can do it about it now."

Shaklin calmed himself, a little sorry that he hadn't called down death and destruction on them all by telling Sten to strike and strike now.

Patience, he told himself. Patience.

Across the room Wichman droned on.

CHAPTER THIRTY FOUR

WHIPSAWED

Sten paced the Control Room while Ida fussed with her com board, flicking this switch and that, tapping keys, palming buttons, but still the com screen connection to the *Flame* remained maddeningly blank.

Across the room, Alex and Doc were hunched over a tall vid-unit, playing Schrodinger's Chess—in 4-D, of course—with pieces winking in and out of existence as the gamers made their moves.

Ida slammed a fist down on her desk, nearly toppling over a nasty-looking cup of caffe with a half-used 'bac stick bobbing on the surface.

"I hate this scrote," she shouted. "Hate him, hate him, hate him."

"What scrote?" Sten asked.

Ida indicated the blank monitor screen. "Why, the nasty little piece of drakh who's keeping our nose out of the *Flame*'s business," she said.

"Do you actually know who he is?" Sten asked.

"Too clottin' right, I know him," Ida said. "Got his puddy paws all over the program. I'd recognize his work anywhere. Except this nasty piece of business has something special. Something so special that it would normally be out of his means to produce it."

"Go on," Sten urged.

Ida shrugged. "Don't know his actual name, but he's a legendary cyber crook. Bragged that there wasn't a wall he couldn't breech, a code he couldn't break. Worked on nothing but sneaky, corporate underworld drakh. Usually for the highest bidder."

Sten frowned. "Any idea who that highest bidder might be in this case?" he wanted to know.

"Sure, I do," I said. "Except, he isn't doing it for money. He's doing it because he has to."

"Explain, please," Sten said.

"Word is that he ran afoul of the Tahn. Got caught with his hand in one of their top secret cookie jars. So they snatched him up and put him to work in one of their labs building drakh to mess with our boss, the Emp."

"Wait, wait, wait," Sten said. "Do you realize what you are saying?"

Ida looked up at him, puzzled. She'd been so focused on the narrow tech picture that she hadn't twigged on what was really going on.

Sten said, "We know for a fact that Venatora is using that program to block us, right?"

Ida nodded. "Right?" Then her face cleared. "Aw, drakh," she said. Then, half-admiringly: "You clever little bitch, you. Went and made yourself a deal with the Tahn."

Her hand went to the cup of caff, saw what was floating inside, and gave it up.

"Well, drakh and fall back in it," she said.

Across the way, Doc and Alex had broken off their game when they caught the Venatora/Tahn reference.

Doc slid off his seat. "We'd better fill Mahoney in about the Tahn," he said.

Sten nodded. "Yeah, we'd better," he said. "This could change everything."

He looked up at the big overhead monitor, where he could see the *Flame* hovering protectively over the circled space-train.

And noted the charred black streak on the tail section where the explosion meant for Sten and Alex had backblasted and scarred the ship.

The only thing left of the *Flame*'s name was the letter "F."

Sten tucked that little bit of detail away, not knowing what use he could make of it, but being careful to file it just the same. In his short but white-hot Mantis career, he'd noticed that little things had a way of growing in importance down the line.

"I just wish I knew what was going on," he said. "We can't even raise the com unit we gave Gregor to talk to his father."

Ida looked up from her board. "It's good news and bad news time," she said.

"I could use some good news about now," Sten said.

She tapped her monitor – a maze of thick red lines, with one green line snaking through.

"That's Shaklin's unit," she said, indicating the green line. "I've managed to at least get through that part of the firewall."

Sten snorted. "Yeah, but is he answering? Or has Mr. Holy Man decided to change sides again?"

"Never fear, young Sten," Kilgour said. "Have faith in our wee bishop. He'll be reporting in any second now."

Sten shook his head. "You only met the guy once, Alex," he said. "Where did all this 'Faith' nonsense come from?"

Soon as the words were out of his mouth, Sten wanted to take them back. But no, Alex grabbed the story opportunity ball and ran with it.

"Ah, told ye', young Sten," he said. "There nothing we Kilgours don't know about faith. Was I not just telling you the tale of th' three holy men—all proud members of the Kilgour clan—took to converting bears?"

Sten started to protest, but Ida, bored and frustrated, broke in. "Yeah, you were telling us about that priest…"

"Aye, Father Kilgour," Alex said.

"Yeah, Father Kilgour. And then there was the minister and the rabbi. What happened to them?"

"Weel," said Alex, "it was loch thes. Efter Father Kilgour tauld his tale, th' Reverend Billy Bob Kilgour wis nae to be ootdain. He was sitting in a wheelchair…hud one puir arm an' both legs in a cast, wi' an IV drip runnin' inae his veins.

"An' in his best fire an' brimstone oratory he shooted, 'Weel, brothers, we Baptists don't sprinkle. We gang whole hog.

"'I went out an' foiund me a bear an' Ah began to reid God's Holy Wuid tae heem. But he didn't want nothin' fur tae do wit' me. An' sa I grabbed heem by th' neck and we began to wrestle somethin' fierce-loch.

"'Weel, me an th' bear rolled doon a big body bare, 'en anither, 'en feel intae a lake. An' Ah quick-loch grabbed his heed an' dunked heem under th' water an' Baptized his hairy soul.

"'An' 'en, when Ah let heem, it was jist loch ye said, Father Kilgour…he was gentle as a wee lamb.'"

Alex paused for dramatic effect. Then opened his mouth to

continue the story, now featuring Rabbi Kilgour, when Ida's monitor suddenly bloomed into life.

And there was Shaklin, his dark features drawn and haggard and he was saying, Captain Sten? Are you there? …Captain Sten?"

Ida did her magic, and suddenly they were in two-way communication.

"I'm here, Bishop Shaklin," Sten said. "What's going on?"

"It's all gone to hell, is what is going on." Shaklin paused. Then—his voice quivering with emotion—he said: "Gregor's getting away with everything."

CHAPTER THIRTY FIVE

BAIT AND SWITCH

"Report!" commanded the ghostly figure that was General Ian Mahoney.

And so Sten reported. Meanwhile, Mahoney paced back and forth in a room that was millions upon millions of light years away.

It could be a gut-wrenching sight, such as when Mahoney paced toward a com desk, then paused midway through it—his big Irish upper body poking above the desk, looking as if he had been cut in half.

When Sten was done, Mahoney hopped back onto a desk in his far away office, leaving the holo image of his booted feet aboard the *Jo'l Cash* dangling over the deck. The sight made Sten's stomach roil.

"This clotting problem just seems to get worse and worse," Mahoney said. "First we learn that Venatora is in cahoots with the bloody Tahn. And now you're saying that Lord Wichman is as well?"

"That's what Shaklin told us, sir," Sten said. "And we have no reason to disbelieve him. Apparently Wichman has been black marketing weapons and forbidden technology to the Tahn for several years now. Including a com hack that can block all communications. When Venatora approached the Tahn with the promise of a whole space-train of Imperium X, they recruited Wichman to act as her go-between."

"I suppose it's because they learned the mutineers were holding his son hostage," Mahoney said. "Gave them more leverage."

"That's our reading, sir," Sten said. Alex, Ida, and Doc murmured agreement.

"But what about our offer?" Mahoney asked, clearly frustrated. "It's so much better than Venatora's. Plus there's the promise of amnesty, damn it! That's a huge clotting concession."

"Wichman's convinced them that it's all a lie," Sten said. "That as soon as they turn themselves in, they'll all be facing firing squads. Meanwhile, Gregor will go free and unpunished for his many sins."

Mahoney was silent for a long, uncomfortable moment.

"What about it, sir?" Sten finally said. "The amnesty offer is legit, right?"

"Sure, sure," Mahoney said, a little too hastily for Sten's comfort.

"And the court martial?"

Mahoney shrugged. "That's always been dicey," he admitted. "His old man..." he let the rest trail off, but Sten took his meaning.

"Yeah, his bigshot old man," Sten said.

"What's their next move?" Mahoney asked. Then he snorted, impatient with himself. "Clot! I know what *their* next move is going be. The question is when, not what."

"In approximately 20 E-hours," Sten said, "They are going to create some sort of diversion. Probably a flash-bang to confuse our communications. Then they are going to make their way to Venatora's base. Her people will guide them through the mine fields."

Mahoney thought a minute, then asked, "How much do you trust this Shaklin fellow?"

"I have a few doubts," Sten admitted, "but I think we can rely on him up to a point."

"And that point would be Gregor?" Mahoney asked. "Because of the death of his beloved Pegatha? Vengeance is mine, sayeth the Church of the Universal Point. And never mind the money? Hmm?"

Kilgour broke in. "Th' wee bishop is ruled by his heart nae his purse. He wants revenge, an' we're th' only ones fa can gie it."

"What about you, Ida?" Mahoney asked.

"I got lost in the purse comparison, boss," she said. "And I'm not known for a soft heart."

"And you, Doc?"

Doc scratched the fur under his chin with a sharp talon. He said, "Although I hate to agree with our haggis-eating friend, I've concluded that Shaklin has been overtaken by the weaker side of his human nature."

He paused, then added, almost under his breath, "As if there were any strong sides."

The holo image of Mahoney hopped off the desk. "Okay, then. We'll proceed on that assumption."

He paused, then said to Sten: "You do have a plan to subvert these beggars, don't you?"

Sten hesitated, then remembered the blackened area on the *Flame*'s tail section. And it all came together.

"I do, sir," Sten said.

"And that plan is?"

"Give me an hour to work out the details, sir," Sten replied. "I'll report back to you."

"Excellent," Mahoney said. "Meanwhile, I'll notify Admiral Gessler to stand by to jump in the moment you send up a flare."

"Very good, sir," Sten said.

And then Mahoney was gone.

Sten turned to see the others staring at him.

"What's this big plan, buster?" Ida asked. "You haven't said anything to us."

"Sorry," Sten said. "I just thought of it."

Everyone relaxed, looking relieved.

Ida said, "Okay, where we do start?"

"I'm working on the premise that the *Flame* and the *Jo 'l Cash* are sister ships," Sten said. "Identical in every way except their names and electronic signatures."

"That, and the big charred tail section on the *Flame*," Ida said.

At that point Kilgour slapped his knee and started laughing.

"What's so funny, Brogue Boy?" Ida demanded.

"Our wee Sten," Alex said. "He's gonna pull a bait and switch."

Ida frowned. Then her brow cleared as she got it. "I'll get busy pawing through the God Box," she said. "Saw some drakh there that'll do the job."

And she slid off her chair and waddled away.

As she left, Doc said in an uncharacteristically plaintive voice: "Will someone please tell me what the clot is going on?"

The only answer—peals of laughter from Kilgour.

CHAPTER THIRTY SIX

VENATORA'S DREAMS

Venatora's plas-domed fortress turned slowly in space, an exotic gem of glimmering lights against a starry backdrop.

This was her most essential outpost, her first, second and last defense against any and all enemies of what she and her Himmenops sisters called "The Colony."

That it was bristling with weapons went without saying. It also possessed the most sophisticated battle computers, com systems, and high tech shields that money could buy on the black market.

They weren't up to Imperial standards, of course, but with the wealth that would soon come pouring in from her latest endeavor, plus her long-term agreements with the Tahn, she'd soon be closer to his level. On this little corner of his Empire, that is.

The fortress sat about a third of the way into the Kill Zone she'd constructed years before and had constantly upgraded with the latest mines and other nasties guaranteed to take down anything up to and including Imperial battleship.

She could wreak enough damage on the nastiest dreadnaught to give a battle-hardened admiral pause. Allowing her more than enough time to fall back behind a series of defenses that would whittle away any force thrown against her.

Making things even more difficult for her enemies was the Armageddon wasteland that was the Possnet Sector.

Back to back ancient celestial disasters had turned everything in the Sector into rubble—ranging from a few planet-sized to billions of smaller particles that whipped about one another in crazy mini-orbits, many ending in collisions that created even more rubble.

Originally, the Himmenops had carved a relatively safe space into the Sector as a means to escape their enemies. Of which they had many. The Himmenops were piratical by nature and darted about the Empire in swift little ships, hijacking whatever they could lay hands on, then retreating into the Colony to enjoy their loot.

With the rise of the Fathers, now led by Father Raggio, and the creation of Venatora, the Colony grew in a grand scale that required more and more space and stolen resources.

It was Venatora's cunning and sheer courage that allowed her to vastly increase the latter, and her organizational skills that led to an even more formidable base of operations, tucked into the middle of a Sector where celestial disturbances and disasters were a regular occurrence.

This, along with her super-enhanced pheromonal powers, kept all her subjects in a state of lustful adoration that she could dial up to a religious frenzy at will.

She and her Fathers had created a place that kept all the chaos that was the Possnet Sector at bay, with gigantic shields that warded off the worst of the disasters. Occasionally her scientists would spot a impending collision that might overwhelm the Colony's shields, and she'd mount mini-expeditions to move the offending planetoid into a safer orbit.

Over the years, several hundred of these planetoids had been hollowed out by Venatora and her Himmenops to create homes, factories, and workshops for her endeavors.

The Himmenops prospered mightily under her rule. Population pressures had already caused the Colony to split once. And it had taken years of stealth and back-court killings before Venatora managed to unite the pirate colonies under her crown.

And now, that time was upon Venatora once again. A new rival had risen. Her name was Princess Anthofelia and she had many supporters of her cause. In the past, Venatora and had been able to keep rival princesses and blasphemers at bay by sheer force of personality, wit and pheromonal dominance. When those failed, she had teams of loyal assassins among her Zabanya guardswomen to eliminate any and all transgressors.

But this time it was different. Her pirate operations had been so successful that it had blown out the natural order of things and the population of the Colony had grown to the point where governing had become unwieldy.

But Venatora was more determined than ever to maintain her iron-handed rule. There could only by one queen of the Himmenops, and Venatora was determined to remain that monarch.

Her new alliance with the Tahn was making all that possible. It didn't matter that she disliked her new allies. They were a cold people, obsessed with warfare, and who had little love of the finer things that life had to offer, like art and music and theater. All of which Venatora supported and encouraged among her own people with lavish grants for the most talented young Himmenops her scouts could find.

"You must always remember, daughter," Father Raggio was wont to say, "that an ally should be looked upon as nothing more than a future vassal state."

Such was the ambition of Raggio and the other fathers who saw no end to the possibilities of Himmenops rule.

And now the greatest coup of her piratical career was only a few E-hours away. Soon, Zheng and Rual would cause the diversion that would fix Sten's attentions on the wrong direction.

Then they would slip away and, relying on the skills of the navigator, Bishop Shaklin, approach the Killing Zone where the first mines would be hidden.

There she would reveal the safe course to them, and they'd weave their way past mines and planetoids bristling with missiles and guns all the way to The Fortress, where Venatora would greet them with open arms.

And she would sweep all that lovely Imperium X into her charge. Then, with the help of the cunning Lord Wichman, she'd sell the entire train for enough credits to drown out Anthofelia and her adherents.

Later, with her influence and voice vastly diminished, one of Venatora's assassins would silence Anthofelia once and for all.

Yes, life was good, she thought. Not perfect, of course, but good.

And then she thought of Sten and felt her loins stir.

Sten. Ah, yes, Sten.

What wonderful daughters they could make together. Daughters worthy of one day ascending the throne to continue Venatora's rule, assuring the future of the Himmenops.

Father Raggio had told her that this was not only a distinct possibility, but one to be greatly desired. One of his minions had scoured the Xypaca area after the fight and had collected Sten's biological spoor.

Samples had been taken and it was Father Raggio's opinion—or, more likely the opinion of his breeding scientists—that Sten had the perfect genetic makeup to add to Venatora's DNA pool.

But that was all very technical and supremely passionless.

Not at all the way Venatora felt about Sten. She wondered what it would be like if they were ever found the opportunity to alone together.

She shivered in anticipation. Promising herself that the day of that assignation would not be too far away.

And then Marta was plucking at her sleeve and speaking with some urgency.

"Ma'am! Ma'am! They're coming, Ma'am!"

Venatora snapped to full attention and examined her vidboard.

It was true. The *Flame* was approaching the Kill Zone.

She frowned. But why were they more than two hours early?

Venatora looked closer.

CHAPTER THIRTY SEVEN

SNOOP AND POOP

Venatora's heart picked up a beat as she watched the distant ship move through the No Being's Zone and near the mines on the outer edges of the Colony.

It was the *Flame*, no doubt about it. She was a light cruiser, of recent vintage. What Jane's "Fighting Star Ships" termed the Radoslaw class. She could see the charred section of the tail—with the ship's name blackened out except for the "F."

The damage was the fault of Rual, that misbegotten fool, who had nearly spoiled her plans by attacking Sten.

Obediently following behind the ship on powerful tractor beams was the 125-kilometer space-train bearing all that Imperium X that the Tahn wanted so badly.

"Got a confirmation on the electronic signature, Ma'am," Marta said. "She's definitely the *Flame*."

She turned to her mistress, worry lines furrowing her brow. "But why is she so early, Ma'am?"

Venatora didn't reply, she just studied the ship with just a niggling of doubt.

"Shall I contact her, Ma'am?" Marta asked, reaching for the com board.

"No!" Venatora snapped. "We must maintain radio silence as agreed. We don't want to alert the Imperials that something is amiss."

There was a hidden buoy at the edge of zone. If the ship was somehow flying under false colors, it would be obliterated when it reached the buoy.

Then she heard was a distinctive series of beeps coming from the com board.

"It's Station Alpha, Ma'am," Marta said. "The missiles are

armed and ready."

"Stand by," Venatora said.

More beeps.

"They're standing by, Ma'am."

Just then the ship slowed, coming very nearly to a halt.

A series of high pitched noises poured forth, in the distinctive long short pattern of the archaic Morse Code she and the mutineers had agreed to use.

.- .-.. .-.. / --- -.- .- -.-- .-.-.- / .-. . --.- ..- . ... - / .--. . .-.
-- .. .. --- -. / - --- / .--. .-. --- -.-. . . -.. .-.-.-

"Translate," Venatora snapped.

"Ma'am, it reads: 'All okay. Request permission to proceed.' Just like we agreed, Ma'am."

Venatora considered. Then: "Signal: 'Permission granted.' And tell Station Alpha to stand down."

A second later Marta reporter, "Station Alpha standing down, Ma'am."

All her doubts vanished. She personally took charge of the board, sending signals to guide the *Flame* through the maze of mines and missiles that guarded The Colony.

ABOARD THE *JO'L CASH*

Sten had cleared the Bridge for an operation that Mahoney warned would likely be declared "Eyes Only" in the very near future.

"We don't want too many people watching how we make sausage," he'd said.

And so the only people with him were Alex, Ida, Doc, Mk'wolf, and two techs who had been TDY'd to Mercury Corps operations a time or three in the past.

"They've got clearances up th' clottin' sheep's whazoo," Alex observed after double-checking their creds.

"What in the clotting clot is a clotting sheep's whazoo," Ida demanded.

Kilgour grinned. "A bit a haggis in the makin'," he said.

Only the two newbies, Warrant Officer Murgas and Warrant

Officer Tm'beaty, laughed.

Sten glared them into silence. It was not good to feed the machine that was Alex Kilgour. You never knew what would set him off into spotted snake land.

Ida and Doc added glares of their own to underscore the point.

Sten turned to the big holomap on the com board. Before Venatora had so rudely shut down their bugs aboard the *Flame*, Ida had carefully copied Shaklin's depiction of Possnet Sector, with the emphasis on Venatora's fortress lair.

As they came to the edge of what Shaklin's map declared a No Being's Zone, He could see a wavery yellow line play between two red points.

"They've got missiles at those points," Ida said, as she guided the *Flame* toward the yellow line.

"Steady," Sten said.

Ida pressed forward.

Then she said, "They're arming the missiles!"

"GA," Sten said.

Ida kept going.

Her eyebrows rose and she said: "they're clottin' painting us!"

"Hold on," Sten said.

Ida held on, hand poised over a "jump" button that would hopefully get them out of harm's way in the nick of a decaying atom.

An odd feeling—a weak electronic tingle—passed through the *Jo'l Cash*. It was as if some Hellhound of a Presence was sniffing them.

"They're checking to see if we're the *Flame* inside as well as out," Ida said.

She leaned back. A little more confident. There was no one in the Mantis Section who could create a better electronic disguise than Ida.

If the charred over painted name on the ship was the *Flame*, then so was every other electronic signature aboard the phantom that was in reality, the *Jo'l Cash* with a tail section bearing a fake wound.

"I think they're satisfied," Ida said. "But there's still a little doubt."

"Transmit the code," Sten said, and seal the deal."

"Aye," Alex said and sent the coded passwords: "permission

to proceed."

The two red dots turned green.

Even so, Sten didn't breathe again until they'd passed the yellow line

AT VENATORA'S FORTRESS

Venatora eased back and stretched out a languid hand. Marta instantly filled it with a Venatora's favorite drink—a mildly fermented mixture of lemon and honey chilled to perfection.

She sipped, examining the *Flame* as it moved through an elaborate maze, the hundred and twenty five kilometer long ore train trailing behind.

Then she frowned. There was something…not…quite…right.

She leaned forward. Eyes scanning the entire length. No. Everything was as it should be. Even so… There was a…*lack*…of something.

And then she realized that what she wasn't seeing was the usual activity that went on outside the *Flame*.

Normally, swarms of little maintenance and repair bots would be sniffing around, looking for any possible breakdowns, or places holed by a meteorite that gotten through the ship's shields.

"Marta," she said, hesitantly. "When was the last time—"

ABOARD THE *JO'L CASH*

"Ah, drakh and clottin' fall back in it!" Ida shouted.

"What's got yer Gypsy knickers in a twist, lass?" Alex asked.

"I forgot the clottin' foofarah," she said, turning to her left and palming a switch.

Immediately, little multi-colored lights starting running up down the board.

"What's that all about?" Sten asked. Should he be worrying?

AT VENATORA'S FORTRESS

Venatora caught herself mid-query when she saw a little bot scurry out from under the damaged tail section.

A few seconds later a whole swarm followed and got busy on other parts of the ship.

"You were saying, Ma'am?" Marta asked.

Venatora waved her away. "Nothing, dear, nothing," she said.

The bots had obviously been busy repairing the damage caused by that fool, Rual. She was ashamed that she shared the same gender as that hot-headed fool.

Pity Venatora was a woman of her word. Otherwise, after the deal had been completed, she would have done everyone a favor and eliminated Rual. And that toad-face Zheng along with her.

Oh, well. She sighed, then savored another sip of her lemon and honey drink.

ABOARD THE *JO'L CASH*

On the holomap, Venatora's fortress looked like nothing more than an great ugly hunk of dirty gray ice.

There were great crater-like cracks running along the surface. Many of the craters seemed to be in permanent shadow.

Ida glanced over at Murgas and Tm'beaty, who were busy doing backup scans of their own.

"Guys?" she asked.

"Black ice," Murgas said.

"Confirmed," said Tm'Beaty.

Ida turned back to Sten. "Perfect camouflage," she said.

Sten nodded. The ice would hide any heat given off by weapons batteries.

Circling the fortress were several smaller ice bodies, orbiting like miniature moons.

"More guns and missiles and mines and bombs and drakh," Ida said, her hands flying across her weapons' board, palming buttons, turning dials and toggling switches.

She checked with Murgas and Tm'Beaty. "Still with me, guys?"

"Affirmative, boss," Murgas said.

"Those are basically sentries," Ida told Sten. "One false move and they'll all open up on us. So, my advice to you, young Sten, is to be very picky about the timing of our false move."

"We can do a lot of damage when we strike," Sten said. "Even crippling damage. But there's no way we can take her out all by our lonesome."

Doc sighed. "Naturally, in human affairs the easiest solution is one you're forbidden to take."

He scratched his furry chin with a single extended claw so

sharp it glittered in the light. "Eventually, our orders are to kill her," he said. "Unfortunately, just not now."

"Aye, we ken only sting 'er," Alex said, "Ain then run loch heel when she sets the dogs oan us."

"Never fear, Ida's here," the fat Rom chortled as she moved a hand across the board.

An area of the Fortress was enlarged and Sten saw a large yellowish hump, like a ripe boil, between two craters.

"What do you make of that?" she asked the techs.

Murgas and Tm'Beaty got busy digging into their data stream.

A minute later, Murgas said, "That's their primary operation center, boss. Take that out and they'll be blind."

But Tm'Beaty was still going at it. "Hang on," he said, fingers hammering away at his board. Turned to Sten. "They've got all kinds of backup, Captain. If we knock that out, in about two seconds flat a whole mess of other systems will come on line."

Ida studied the stream. Nodded. "In other words," she said, "all hell will break loose."

Doc broke in. "I calculate that it's more than just an operation center," he said. "I've come to admire Venatora's cunning. And it is my observation that she's purposely put an attractive target in plain view."

Sten chuckled. God, he admired that woman.

"Bait for a trap," he said.

"A wee bit of cheese for th' rats," Alex said.

Ida's hands began flying across her board again. "I'll look for a better clottin' target," she said.

"Hold on," Sten said. "Considering our purpose, we have already found it."

Ida frowned. "What are you thinking?"

"That we grab the cheese and then run like hell," Sten said. "And do as much damage as possible on the way out."

He turned to Murgas and Tm'Beaty. "I want you to sus out all possible danger areas," he said. "When the drakh hits the fan, I want to know the most likely places the attacks will come from."

Then to Ida: "Take out everything they throw at us. But don't get too antsy. I want Venatora to have plenty of muscle left when we get to Stage Two of this little operation."

And now to Alex. "I know you've got the escape route mapped

out," he said. "But I'm not fooling myself Venatora won't try to close that off before we can shake free."

"Nae a problem, laddie," Alex said. "Ah've got uir wee jump point primed an' ready tae gang."

"And how about you, Doc?" Sten said. "You've been in constant contact with Shaklin. How is he holding up?"

"Better than I expected," Doc said. "In fact, he's so calm that I wonder if he has something else planned."

"Do you think he'll turn on us at the last minute?" Sten asked.

"Not as yet," Doc said. "Just be warned to expect the unexpected."

"Tha's th' Kilgore clan's first rule ay war," Alex said. "If things can go wrang, you'd best coont on it."

Sten moved over to Ida's side.

"Ready?"

She laughed. "Now comes my favorite part," she said.

"And what would that be?"

"You say 'Fire.'"

"Okay, then," Sten said. "Fire!"

Ida stabbed a fat finger at the button.

CHAPTER THIRTY EIGHT

ALL HELL BREAKS LOOSE

A smile spread across Venatora's face as the *Flame* moved closer to her fortress. Soon all that lovely Imperium X would be hers.

She keyed the mike and was about to hail the ship when saw the gunports suddenly yawn open, there was a flash, and a blazing white flare consumed the entire screen. A tremendous force hit the fortress, and she was nearly hurled from her seat.

As if from afar, she heard Marta cry out, "What're they doing? They're attacking! They're attacking!"

Distantly, she could hear other guardswomen shouting. Now came another explosion, and then alarms were blaring and all she could think was that she had been a fool.

The Emperor had tricked her. The mutiny. The theft of the Imperium X. The traitorous conspiracy of Lord Wichman and his son. It was nothing but an elaborate ruse to get her to let down her guard.

And now the Imperial forces would be on her, intent on killing her and destroying The Himmenops Colony.

Cold fury descended, and then an odd kind of calm. She slowly rose, turning up the volume of her power over her women, and soon restored order.

The order remained as a series of jolts rocked the fortress. Her automated defense systems were working and striking back. But unless she moved fast, it might well prove to be too little and too late. Any second now other Imperial forces would join the *Flame* and wreak destruction on The Colony.

Then Marta shouted that she had reestablished a connection to the outside. Venatora looked up as two guardswomen hoisted a new monitor into place. It blinked to life.

The sight jolted her. What was this?

Venatora expected to see the *Flame*, accompanied by an Imperial fleet, bearing down on her, chain guns blazing, missile bays aflame. But instead the only thing to appear on the screen was the *Flame*.

Except it wasn't attacking!

It was clotting running away!

The charred tail section clearly outlined as it fled a barrage of counter missiles that her automated batteries had unleashed.

And where was the Imperium X? The hundred and twenty five kilometer ore train had simply vanished, as if it had never existed.

Well, of course! She kicked herself for not realizing it before.

They'd hardly risk something so incredibly valuable to bait the trap. She was sure that the after action reports would reveal that the ore train was nothing more than an electronic phantom. Had this always been the case? Had the Imperium X ever existed at all?

Venatora shook off those questions. Silly speculation that should be left for another time.

She would pour it on, by God! She would make them pay!

Venatora issued a stream of orders, and her guardswomen sprang into action. Missiles launched. Mines moved into action. The screen filled with fiery objects all aimed at the departing *Flame*.

"Shall I scramble the squadron, Ma'am?" Marta asked.

Within seconds, she could send a score of her best Crossbow fighters into the fray. They were small, two-women vessels, but had enough firepower to overmatch ships three times their size. And at their controls were her very best pilots—Zabanya hardened fighters with countless successful ship-boardings to their credit.

Venatora was about to order them into action when it suddenly occurred to her that maybe—just maybe—this is exactly what the Imperials wanted her to do

She had no doubt that Sten's fingerprints were all over this. The cool trickery he had displayed during the Xypaca debacle was just a small example of just how cunning he could be.

Fury almost overtook her again. He couldn't hide behind that cocky grin. He was cheating her and enjoying himself immensely while doing it!

"Ma'am? Ma'am?" It was Marta.

Venatora took breath. Cooled herself. Squared her shoulders. "No," she said. "Stand down."

Marta gaped at her. "But, Ma'am—" she stared, but Venatora cut her off with a raised hand.

"That was just a feint," Venatora said. "The Imperials were testing our defenses. But, rest assured, they will be back. In full force. Next time, we will be ready!"

ABOARD THE *JO'L CASH*

On the holomap, Sten could see they were approaching the outer edges of Venatora's pirate kingdom. Beyond lay the No Being's Land and safety.

He braced himself, fully expecting to be met by all the firepower Venatora had at her command.

Tm'beaty was standing by, ready to unleash thick clouds of electronic flak to confound Venatora's missile batteries.

Meanwhile, Murgas was primed to take out any missiles that happened to break through.

Ida was using all her skills to retrace the route through the minefield and Kilgour was online with Shaklin, keeping the bishop apprised of everything that was going on.

Doc, of course, was being Doc. Sitting with his paws crossed across his furry little paunch like a miniature Buddha, reviewing everything that had happened and analyzing how everyone had behaved.

Sten turned to Murgas and Tm'beaty. "Report," he said.

Murgas shook his head. "Nada, Captain. Just that initial barrage, then it stopped."

"Same here, Captain," Tm'beaty said. "Figured she'd be trying to turn us into toast right about now."

Sten glanced at Kilgour, who was listening to whatever Shaklin had to say. He gave Sten a thumb's all. All was well.

"How about you, Ida?" Sten asked.

"Zip, zero, zed," she said. "They're quiet as little mousies over there."

He nodded at the furry Buddha. "What's your reading, Doc?"

"Right about now," he said, "she's kicking herself for being all kinds of a fool."

"Sure, but why the silence? The non action? I figured she'd be pouring it on. Giving us all kinds of hell."

"Which we are prepared for," Ida said, with a nasty smile. "Boy, did I have some surprises for her."

"Even so," Sten said. "She might have gotten in a lucky shot."

"She's double thinking us," Doc said. "That's her Achilles heel."

He glanced over at Ida. "Or, her *tell*, as our gypsy friend would put it.

Ida snorted and shot Doc a middle finger.

Dock turned back with the air of a cat who had amused himself with a mouse.

"Venatora's double-think habit has led her to believe that we are wiggling our netherparts to draw an attack. And that we have another trick up our—"

He stopped. Looked at his furry paw. Wiggled it. Flashed his fangs in amusement. Then said, "Well, you get the idea."

Sten chuckled. "Well, she's right about the trick business," he said. "It's just not the trick she's expecting."

He looked over at the holomap. They'd crossed into No Beings Land. And safety.

Sten breathed a sigh of relief. Not for himself, but for Venatora.

He hadn't been forced to kill her, Mahoney or no Mahoney.

CHAPTER THIRTY NINE

THE BISHOP AND THE RABBI

Shaklin and his two top Navtechs, Viktor and Newton, moved quietly through the huge tractor-beam chamber. A low hum came from immense machines lined up in long corridors that bisected the chamber. Massive as they were, they made only a low thrumming sound. The deck beneath Shaklin's feet trembled with their power.

It was their purpose to link all the immense oar cars together until they formed a hundred and twenty five kilometer train. Which, in turn was linked to the *Flame* by a web of high energy Trac-beams.

He came to the main board, then waved Newton forward. Over the years Shaklin had all his congregants trained in multiple shipboard skills. Newton excelled at tractor-beam technology.

All the calculations had been made in advance, so it only took Newton a few minutes to make the necessary adjustments. When done, he stepped back.

"The minute I give the word," Shaklin said, "it's your job to blow the main connection."

"We won't let you down, eminence," Newton said.

They moved down the bank of controls to another position, Shaklin's beaded dreadlocks clattering in the deep silence.

"I calculate that we can Trac twenty nine cars without overburdening the *Caird*," Shaklin said.

Newton nodded, finger moving over the board. He started counting from the last ore car forward: "One…two…three…" until he reached 29. Then he flipped a switch to mark the Trac connection. Slid a little tube from his pocket and aimed it at the switch. Pressed a button. Light flash. Tiny curl of smoke.

He stepped back. "That's a good job done, eminence," he said with satisfaction.

Shaklin clapped him on the shoulder. "Excellent," he said. "Now to tie it all together."

And he led Newton and Viktor deeper into the chamber.

The tractor beam chamber occupied the *Flame*'s stern and the emergency escape craft was stowed there. It was a cunning little boat, which Shaklin had dubbed the *Caird* after a vessel that an ancient explorer had used to rescue his ice-bound crew in one of old Earth history's great navigational feats.

The *Caird* wasn't large enough to rescue more than a third of the *Flame*'s crew in a real disaster. But it was more than sufficient for Shaklin's needs. He only had nineteen beings in his charge, all faithful members of the Church of the Universal Location.

He and his congregants had stuffed every conceivable space with enough supplies to last for several months, along with weapons and ammunition, which he would only use as a last resort.

Plus, there was one other thing—a lifeboat—that they needed to get on board. It had taken days for Shaklin and his people to move the lifeboat from section to section without other crew members spotting them and asking what they were up to.

The little vessel was only large enough for two beings and had barely enough air to last a couple of hours. But that was sufficient for his needs. Besides, he only required space for one being, not two.

In not too long he'd take the controls of the *Flame* and begin the countdown for what Zheng had proclaimed "Zee Beeg Clottin' Run." To do that they'd need a diversion to occupy Sten and the Imperial sailors aboard the *Jo 'l Cash* until the *Flame* slipped away.

First, they'd slowly build the ship's engines to full life.

Then Rual and her weapons techs would launch a barrage of missiles at the *Jo 'l Cash*. They had no hope of actually hitting the ship. The Imperial Navy crew would spot the threat before the first missile cleared the *Flame*'s gunports. But there would be a whole lot of "Flash and Drakh and Boom," as Rual put it, "and then you clottin' go, Bishop! Clottin' go!"

She'd tried to loom over Shaklin to press her point, but he just stared her down, then turned and coolly gave instructions to his people. Angry but satisfied, Rual stormed off.

And so when Rual said, "Go!" he'd give the *Flame* full power then blast toward Venatora's fortress.

Assuming the *Jo'l Cash* was still busy with the flash bang, they'd reach No Being's Land intact. Then, they just had to wait for Venatora's signal to proceed, and it would be Shaklin's final task to guide the *Flame* through the warren of mines and missile batteries to their buyer.

That's how it was supposed to work. That's how Zheng, Rual and Venatora had planned it.

But that's not what was going to happen.

"Get ye ready to jump, laddie," Kilgour had warned. "Soon as Venatora hears your voice, she'll blow ya to smithereens. Or, cause she's such a canny lass, she may let wait until you are well on your way, getting your hopes up, and then you'll smash you down with all th' hot metal and bombs she can muster."

Shaklin felt remarkably calm after hearing this. He let Kilgore's words pour over him and suddenly he could see the future clear.

If not to the very end of it all.

Or, more aptly, the beginning.

That perfect point.

In that perfect location.

The Grail at the end of his people's search.

No. Probably not.

But it might be close, brother. It might be gloriously close.

Then they were at the *Caird*, and Shaklin sent Viktor aboard to set up the connection with the 29 oar cars he intended to commandeer.

His job done, Viktor was just exiting the little vessel when Rual's high-pitched voice crackled over the speakers.

"Shaklin? Where the clot are you, Shaklin? We need you. Right now."

Shaklin keyed his mike. "Be with you in a minute," he said.

Rual hissed back: "I didn't say in a minute. I said *now*."

Shaklin didn't bother replying. If Rual wanted the last word, let her have it.

Because the last laugh would be his and his alone.

Before they exited the chamber he paused long enough to send Kilgour one final message.

All were systems were definitely go!

Alex listened to Shaklin's report, then wished him good luck and signed off.

"Our wee bishop says to get ready for the flash bang," Kilgour told the others.

Sten turned to Murgas and Tm'beaty. "You boys deal with the incoming," he said.

"Shouldn't be a problem, Captain," Murgas said. "Shaklin's fed us all the coordinates, so we'll be able to track missiles the second they're launched."

"If one of them gets through," Tm'beaty said, "we'll smother them with a big fat cloud of flak. They'll either blow in place or latch on to the nearest large body and chase it into the nearest sun."

Doc called Sten over. "I just got off the com with Admiral Gessler," he said. "He's moving his fleet in closer. I stressed in my most persuasive tones that when we say 'clotting pounce,' he'd better clotting pounce."

"Just so long as the mutineers don't spot him too early," Sten said.

"No worries with Gessler," Ida broke in. "He won't dilly dally. One of my boy toys served with him. Said he had a good rep as a fighting man."

Kilgore ignored all this. He was plainly bored and anxious to get moving. He yawned and gave an elaborate stretch.

Which gave young Murgas the nerve to speak up. Rather hesitantly, he said: "Mr. Kilgour, sir?"

Kilgour turned his cheery face on the lad. "What is it, me boy?"

"About those holy men?"

Kilgour frowned. "Holy men?" Then he remembered and blessed Murgas with broad grin.

"Ay, you mean the three Kilgour holy men," he said. "Father Kilgour. The Right Reverend Billy Bob Kilgour. And Rabbi Kilgour."

Sten groaned and almost intervened, but Murgas looked so hopeful, he didn't have the heart.

"Yessir," Murgas said. "You told us about the first two holy men and how they converted the bears, but you never said what happened to the third Kilgour—the Rabbi."

"Weel," Alex drawled, "if you remember proper, the priest and th' minister were pretty banged up from preachin' to those bears."

Murgas nodded. He remembered.

"But that was nothing compared to what happened to th' wee rabbi," Kilgour said. "Two ambulance drivers carried him into th' pub on a stretcher.

"And he was in a full cast, with traction cables, and IV tubes running into his poor body and monitors beeping news of his vitals, which were weak as clot." Kilgour's face grew sad. He shook his head. "He didn't look long for this world.

"The other holy men begged him to tell them what happencd. How did the bear manage to hurt him so? And poor Rabbi Kilgour peered up at his friends and said, 'Looking back on it, circumcision may have not been th' wisest way to start."

Dead silence filled the chamber.

Tm'beaty and Murgas turned deathly pale when they realized that Kilgour was done. There was no more.

Murgas gagged a little as if he were going to lose his lunch.

Sten gave him a pitying look. "Bet you don't do that again," he said.

Murgas shook himself like a wet dog. Tm'beaty snorted disgust. "If he does," he said, "request permission, sir, to blow him away."

"Permission granted," Sten said.

And then blinding lights filled the overhead screens, and Ida announced, "It's show time, folks!"

CHAPTER FORTY

AND THEN THE KNIVES CAME OUT

As they approach No Being's Land, Shaklin kept an eye peeled at what was going on behind the *Flame*.

It made a tableaux worthy of a billion credit star-packed livee. Missiles streaking. Rockets exploding. Laser guns so hot they warped space.

"If just one leetle missile gets through," he was telling Rual, "maybe real lucky ve get and kill that bastard Sten."

Rual grimaced. "It's Kilgour I want," she said. "And not a missile, but a knife to the throat."

Zheng snorted. Took a swig from his ever present flask, his flushed toad face turning a deeper shade of red.

"Never mind this Sten," he said. "By the bokos we got him. And soon very rich we will be."

Just about then the holomap brightened and Shaklin saw that they were approaching the very edge of Venatora's realm.

On the map, they were coming upon a thin yellow line, that stretched between two red points.

He slowed his approach.

"Vhat doing you?" Zheng demanded.

Shaklin pointed at the yellow line and the two red dots.

"If we cross that line without permission," he said. "We're dead."

Rual cursed Zheng under her breath for being so stupid.

Zheng flared at Shaklin as if it were all his fault.

"Vell, the signal you send then," he say. "Vy are you waiting?"

He sent the signal.

AT VENATORA'S FORTRESS

Venatora smiled as she saw the *Flame* approach her border.

"I knew he'd come," she said to Marta. "It's just the kind of trick Sten would play."

She thought back about their first encounter at the Xypaca fights. He'd tricked her twice. She knew this now for certain. It made her angry, on one level, but on another she admired his cunning. And his willingness to bet it all on a single outcome, trusting that he could outthink any opponent in mid fight.

And here he was again. With the *Flame*. The ore train stretched behind it.

Sure, it was. She snorted.

Venatora didn't bother to ask Marta to sweep the ship or the train. She knew what was real and what wasn't.

Now Sten would have his toady, Zheng, pretend that it had all been a big misunderstanding. Some trick the nasty Imperials had pulled. Zheng would talk, talk, talk, in that backwards language he used, driving her crazy.

Marta broke in. "They're signaling us."

Venatora settled back. Waiting for the verbal river of excuses that Sten—via his mouthpiece, Zheng—would pour upon her.

Marta signaled the *Flame* to stand by, then turned to Venatora.

"They're requesting permission to proceed, Ma'am," she said.

Venatora bolted up. "What? That's it? Permission to proceed? Nothing more?"

Marta was taken aback by her heat. Hesitantly, she said, "No, Ma'am. I mean, yes, Ma'am. That's all there was. 'Permission to proceed.'"

Venatora glared at the board. Wanting to reach right through it and grab Zheng by the throat. Or, better, yet. Sten. Oh, she'd love to lay hands on him.

"Ma'am?" Marta said. "How should I reply, Ma'am?"

Venatora looked at Marta. Forced calm. Then smiled.

"Tell them," she began. "Tell them... Permission granted."

And then Venatora sent the prearranged signal to her forces: *Get ready to open fire.*

ABOARD THE *FLAME*

Shaklin's com board lit up. Venatora's replay was clear: "Permission granted. You may proceed."

As he reached for the controls, Zheng was shouting, "Vhat are you waiting for, you, you stupid? Go!"

Shaklin bit back an angry retort—what the clot did Zheng think he was doing? Instead, he calmly worked the controls, sending the *Flame* smoothly forward.

He glanced over at Viktor and Newton. They nodded at him. All was in readiness.

A moment later, the red points turned green and the *Flame* was moving over the yellow line, through the deadly maze of mines and missile batteries.

His heart hammered a staccato beat. Icy prickles ran up and down his spine. Any second now and Venatora would attack. He was sure of it. He practically felt her anger radiating from the gray fortress. Thoughts of vengeance coming to a boil. Pent up wrath waiting to be unleashed.

She'd pour down so much molten metal and bombs and nuke-tipped missiles that it would be impossible for them to escape.

He heard Zheng chortling. "Soon rich we be," he was telling Rual.

Greeted by gleeful laughter from Rual, so high-pitched she sounded like a mad woman.

Shaklin caught Newton's eye. Mouthed the words, "Get ready." Newton smiled, but he was so frightened it looked more like a rictus grin than anything else.

He could see beads of sweat running down Viktor's face. The other congregants were as equally intense. Lips trembling. Up-turned faces pale with fear.

Any minute now… Any minute…

AT VENATORA'S FORTRESS

"Kill them!" Venatora shouted, slamming her hand down on the com board. "Kill them all!"

And in less than a heartbeat, the entire bank of overhead monitors blazed with missile fire.

ABOARD THE *FLAME*

Shaklin was almost too late. He saw the flame of the first missile and his hand went for the "jump" button, but he was so frightened his hand felt paralyzed.

He reached. But it was slow. So slow.

And Zheng was shouting: "Betrayal!"

And Rual was screaming: "Venatora, you thieving bitch!"

The first missile exploded just short of the *Flame*'s shield! The ship rocked.

Monitors burst and loose material scattered across the Control Center.

And there! Over there! He could see other missiles on their way. Coming… Coming… Coming…

Shaklin punched the "Jump" button. There was a sudden feeling of emptiness.

Disorientation.

And he was falling. Falling.

Then, with a jolt and a shudder, the *Flame* came to a halt.

Dizzily, Shaklin looked around. Zheng had hit his head and he was bleeding. Rual was picking herself off the deck. Crew members cursed. Some were weeping. Others were asking the unanswerable—what do they do now?

Shaklin came to his senses. A great calmness descended.

Newton said, "Here they come."

And he looked up at the holomap and saw half-a-dozen points of lights moving on the *Flame*.

"Imperials," Viktor confirmed. "A whole clotting fleet."

And all could see that they were led by the *Jo'l Cash*.

Shaklin turned to Zheng, who was trembling with fear. Numbly, he upended his flask. Drained it. Threw it aside.

"I guess we're not going to be rich after all," Shaklin said dryly—addressing Newton and the others, but loud enough for all to hear.

"And as for amnesty—" He shook his head. No more needed to be said. That deal was long gone, thanks to the betrayal of Zheng and Rual.

He gave Newton the signal, reached under the rim of his board, and flipped a switch. There was a jolt. The ore train had all but been cut loose. One more step and it would be separated from the *Flame*.

But, jolt or not, no one noticed. For sudden fury had enveloped the crew.

They turned on Zheng and Rual, shouting. "We had a deal! Money! Amnesty! Gone! All gone!"

Zheng tried to grab Shaklin by his tunic. "Jump," he screamed. "Jump! We must escape!"

Shaklin shook his head. "There's no escaping the Eternal Emperor," he said. "His people will follow us to the ends of Uttermost Space and back again."

He turned to the angry crew. Pointing an accusing finger at Zheng and Rual. "It's their fault," he said. "Their doing. They bet your lives that they could out-think the Emperor, and they lost."

Which was a lie. The rest of the crew had all been blinded by greed and by Zheng and Rual's double dealing. They had out-voted Shaklin and his congregants, who were in favor of taking up Sten's offer.

But none of that mattered now. Blame needed to be placed. And when that happens, blame cannot be denied.

"We can still escape," Rual was saying. "We can still jump. Hide out and make a deal later on. Can't we Zheng?"

But Zheng wasn't answering. He was too busy spewing his guts on the deck.

Rual started toward Shaklin. Drawing her knife.

"Jump, damn you!" she demanded. "Jump!"

But Shaklin just turned to his board, grasped the jump switch. Twisted this way and that. And then ripped it right off the board.

He threw it into Rual's face.

"You jump," he said.

He turned and started away. Rual screamed and came after him. Shaklin didn't bother ducking or dodging. It wasn't necessary.

The crew exploded in fury. Some grabbed Zheng, who went down under a pile of punching, tearing bodies. Others went for Rual. Shaklin didn't doubt that she put a good fight. He heard her cries of defiance behind him as he and his congregants exited the Control Room.

Rual's final shout echoed in his ears: "I'll kill you all! Cut your mother humping throats from ear to ear—"

And then there were whispers of sharp steel all around the Control Room as the crew drew knives and advanced on her.

As the door slid shut, he heard her scream, long and loud and full of terrible agony.

At that moment Shaklin learned something new about himself. He quite enjoyed her scream.

CHAPTER FORTY ONE

THE TASTE OF VENGEANCE

Shaklin and his people reached Gregor's cabin. The guards were gone—probably back at the Control Center gleefully helping murder Zheng and Rual.

Newton broke the lock, and Viktor and several others hauled Gregor out.

He was frightened. And more than a little confused.

"What's happening?" he demanded. "Is Venatora coming? Should I call my father so we can finalize the deal?"

Shaklin laughed. "There is no deal," he said. "There never was a deal."

And with immense satisfaction he said, "Now, come with us."

Gregor tried to protest. But Newton and Viktor, who were large enough to handle several Gregors, took him in tow and hustled him along the corridor.

"Where are we going?" Gregor demanded.

No one bothered answering.

A moment later they were in the Tractor Beam Chamber. Newton hurried to the control board, popped it open, and fiddled with the switches. Then he set the timer.

He grinned at Shaklin. "Ten minutes, Bishop. And we'll be clotting out of here."

Meanwhile, Gregor grew more and more frantic.

"Please, please," he was saying. "Just let me call my father. He'll fix it. He can fix anything."

But they were at the *Cairn* now, and Shaklin's people boarded the little vessel, taking up the positions and duties he'd drilled into them. There hadn't been much time, but the members of the Church of the Universal Location were not just devoted, but intelligent, highly trained technicians.

As Shaklin took up his post at the control board, Newton and Viktor hustled Gregor over to the lifeboat, which sat next to a launch tube just large enough to do the job.

He was arguing. Begging. Pleading. But no one paid him any mind.

Shaklin's fingers flew over the controls. Big bay doors opened in front of the *Cairn*. He gave the boat a little power, and they slipped out of the *Flame* into space.

"Like bacon through a goose," Viktor observed.

And now they were skimming along the ore train, heading toward the end of the 129 kilometer line.

Well, the end sans twenty nine cars they were cutting out for themselves. Shaklin grinned at the thought.

Don't get over confident, he warned himself. He had to play each card perfectly. One mistake and all would be lost.

At last the ten minutes were up and a small explosion came where the train linked to the ship. The cars broke away, slowly drifting to the side from the force of the explosion.

Then they were in position. Newton did his magic and there was another small explosion, separating the last twenty nine cars from the train.

Shaklin guided the *Cairn* into place, latched on, then moved away—carrying the mini-train laden with precious Imperium X with him.

It was time to call Sten.

Oh, wait. Not just yet. Gregor first. Then Sten.

"Get him into the boat," he told Newton and Viktor.

Gregor started, but the two big men grabbed him from either side and hustled him to the little lifeboat.

"Wait a minute," Gregor said. "What are you doing?"

"Returning you to your father, what else?" Shaklin said.

"But...but..." he pointed at the lifeboat. "Not in that!"

Shaklin shrugged. "It's for your own protection," he said.

And it wasn't that much of a lie. At this moment he was more than capable of doing Gregor great bodily harm.

"No, no. You must let me go. The Court Martial. They might... they might..."

"Shoot you?" Shaklin asked with a bitter laugh. "A firing squad is too good for you. But that was my agreement with Sten."

Gregor's face turned fiery red. "Sten? Why, he's nothing but a poseur. Acts like an ordinary guy, but he's got connections. That's for sure. Connections he's been lying about for years."

"I'm glad to hear that," Shaklin said. "Makes me even more confident that you have a firing squad in your future."

"Wait, wait, wait," Gregor pleaded. "We can still make this work. We can still do a deal. You can still be rich."

Shaklin had enough. "Get him in there," he said, jabbing a finger at the lifeboat.

Newton opened the little boat's port, and he and Viktor grabbed Gregor and pushed him toward it. Gregor struggled mightily, but Newton gave him a hard swat and Gregor stopped struggling.

Now he was weeping.

"But why?" he pleaded. "Why are you doing this to me?"

Shaklin stared hard into his eyes. "Pegatha," was all he said. He nodded for Newton and Viktor to continue.

They stuffed him, weeping, into the little boat. As they closed the port, the last thing Shaklin heard him say was, "It was an accident, I tell you. Just an accident."

But Shaklin felt no vengeful joy when he turned back to the control board. Instead, he felt empty. And there was a bitter taste in his mouth.

Then he keyed his mike. Time to call Sten.

CHAPTER FORTY TWO

SHAKLIN'S OFFER

Sten gaped at what the big overhead monitor was showing him.

On one side was the *Flame*, separated from the ore train, which was floating slowly away. On the other side, a small vessel—a rescue craft, he guessed—was moving swiftly off, towing a short string of ore cars behind it.

"What the—"

And then Shaklin was on the line. "It's all set, Sten," he was saying. "Zheng and Rual are probably dead by now, and the crew so demoralized I doubt they'll give you any trouble when board."

"We had an agreement, Bishop," Sten said through gritted.

"And I kept it," Shaklin said. Then Sten heard something—was it a little laugh. "Well, most of it, anyway."

"Where's Gregor?" Sten demanded. "You agreed to keep him safe and deliver him to me."

"Oh, Gregor, that's right. You wanted Gregor. Hang on a second."

And Sten saw vapor puff at the little vessel's port, and a small cylinder slipped out of it. It looked like a lifeboat.

Another vapor puff, this time at the rear of the lifeboat and it started moving toward the *Jo'l Cash*.

Then Shaklin returned. "There you go," he said. "One son of a bitch heading your way."

Sten started to protest, but Shaklin kept going. "The thing is, Sten, there is only about two hours worth of oxygen in that thing. So, you'd better move fast if you want to pick Gregor up before he suffers a well-deserved, rather nasty death."

Now Sten understood. Kilgour's wee bishop had played his cards well. If Sten chased Shaklin down, Gregor would die. If he rescued Gregor first, Shaklin would be long gone.

Sten didn't bother struggling for an answer. Mahoney had been quite clear. The Emperor wanted Gregor back. But he also wanted the ore train.

Sten looked over the little string following the *Cairn*. "How many cars are you taking with you?" he asked.

"Twenty nine," Shaklin replied. "Enough to fund our church's good works, but not so much that your boss will want to spend a lot of effort hunting us down."

"I wouldn't bet on that," Sten said. "The Eternal Emperor isn't known for his forgiving nature."

"Let's put it this way, then," Shaklin said. "He was willing to spend enough credits to fund the operations of a small planet to get the ore train back. And I'm doing it for a whole clot of a lot less."

Sten could see his point, but didn't reply.

"Well, I suppose you'd better get to it, Sten," Shaklin said. "Assuming you still want Gregor alive."

Sten started to sigh, which turned into a laugh.

"Good luck to you, Bishop," he said.

"And to you, Sten," Shaklin replied.

Then the image that was the *Cairn* began shiver. It grew thinner and thinner.

And then simply vanished.

Shaklin had made the jump.

To where only the congregants of the Church of the Universal Location knew.

"Better pick Gregor up," Sten instructed Ida.

He turned to Kilgour. "What do you think of your faithful bishop, now, Alex, old buddy, old pal?"

Kilgour grinned. "For him, a wee bit of circumcision worked a charm," Kilgour said.

CHAPTER FOURTY THREE

GHOSTS

Venatora was in an evil mood as she paced the gymnasium, watching her guardswomen go through their paces.

They were her Zabanyans—the best of the best in the entire Himmenops Colony—and they were nearly naked, gloriously so. Heavily muscled but curvaceous. Their skin shone with perspiration.

Trainers took them through one combat position to the next, working with Shaolin whips and canes, edged weapons, and bare fists and feet.

The guardswomen worked with a will, their passions and devotion stoked by Venatora's pheromonal fires.

Normally, she took great joy at times like these. Working with her women, feeling their love and devotion and—yes—lust. It was normally a delicious feeling. But now she felt hollow and empty.

And, if she were honest with herself, a bit like a fool.

Sten had tricked her yet again. He'd pushed her into double think, then added yet another twist that left her empty-handed. This, after draining her treasury to fund the scheme.

But then Marta was suddenly at her side, trying to get her attention.

"Ma'am," she said. "Ma'am."

Venatora nearly snapped, but none of this was Marta's fault. The blame was on Venatora, no one else.

"What is it, dear?" she asked.

Marta flushed, then handed her a com unit.

"An call, Ma'am," she said.

Venatora frowned. "A call? Who is it?"

"It's Bishop Shaklin, Ma'am," Marta said. "He says it's urgent."

And for the first time in many gloomy hours, Venatora smiled.

"I suppose it is," she said, taking the com unit. "Now, let's see what our lovely holy man has to say for himself."

* * * *

Sten perched on the bar stool, a shot of stregg and a narcobeer in front of him. It was a loud bar, a crowded bar—filled with Imperial sailors either going on leave, returning from leave, or in transit to another posting.

Sten had a hand on the stool next to him, saving it for Alex, who had joined the long line waiting to get into the jakes.

"You can usually hold it longer than that," Sten teased before he left."

"What ken Ah say," Kilgour bemoaned. "Me pucker string's busted." And off he went.

At the present, Sten wasn't all that pleased with the State of Things. Sure, Mahoney had said they'd pulled off a big success. There had been promotions all around—Sten was an actual captain, now. With promises of challenging postings.

But, once again, Mahoney had put on things on a "temporary hold." They might be needed for one more mission.

Sten shrugged. That was life in the military. Ho hum. What else is new? Pointless to complain.

He knew nothing of the fate of the mutineers. Probably all dead, or on their way to that state, he thought. They'd blown any chance for amnesty when they tried to sneak off to the enemy.

Besides, Sten had his doubts that amnesty was ever really on, no matter what Mahoney said. If everything was supposed to be hush-to-the-nth degree—hush, then the only way to guarantee it was to make sure the mutineers never talked.

As for Shaklin, God bless him—if there was a God, which Sten strongly doubted. He hoped he would someday find whatever Promised Land his people believed in.

Location point? What was that all about?

He lifted the shot glass to toss it back when he felt a round, soft haunch nestle into the bar stool next to him. With it came the scent of lemon and honey.

Sten turned, thinking if the perfume looked as good the woman smelled and her thigh felt, then Alex was on his own. He could find another place at the bar.

But before he could turn all the way, he felt a little thrill, heard a faint buzz, and a deliciously warm feeling stole over him.

And then he found himself looking at the ebony beauty that was Venatora.

Her lips moist. Eyes deep and dark and glistening. Breath like a heady wine.

She said, "How's my poor soldier boy? Got another hundred thousand credits to bet?"

Sten was taken aback. What did she…then he saw that she was looking at him very much like he was looking at her.

The flushed face. The moist, slightly parted lips. The glistening eyes. It was no act. They were all meant for him.

At that moment the world vanished and all he could think or feel was Venatora.

* * * *

And Venatora thought, If only. If only. But what she said was, "I said that the next time I saw you, I'd kill you." She shrugged. "I guess I lied."

She reached over and took his shotglass. Hoisted it.

"Cheers," she said.

Sten lifted his narcobeer mug.

"Cheers," he replied.

They touched glasses. Then drained them.

"But next time…"

Sten frowned. "Next time—what?"

Instead of answering, Venatora leaned forward until their faces were mere centimeters apart. Her eyes were huge—melting. And he could feel a delicious heat rising up from her body. Enveloping him.

He reached for her. Venatora let him touch one perfect ebony cheek. Her lush lips parted.

And they kissed.

* * * *

It was a long kiss. Sten felt like he was submerged in a warm, dark river of sensations.

He reached with his other hand, meaning to embrace her.

Venatora placed a gentle hand on his chest and firmly pushed him away.

Sten tried to speak. But all he could manage was a strangled croak.

Then, somehow he managed: "Venatora. We must—"

Two fingers touched his lips, silencing him.

And she said, "We shall, Sten. We shall."

She slid off the stool and stepped away.

Sten tried to follow, but before he could get to his feet she was gone. Lost in the crowd.

He felt a hand on his shoulder. He turned. It was Alex. His friend started to speak, then stopped and looked at him.

"What's happened, lad?" he asked. "You look like you've gone and seen a ghost."

"I think I just did," Sten said.

He turned back to the bar. God, he needed a drink.

CHAPTER FORTY FOUR

AN IMPERIAL DECREE

When Mahoney entered the Eternal Emperor's study, he didn't quite know what to expect.

The young Gurkha officer who'd come to fetch him gave no hint, but only stood, impatiently shifting from foot to foot as Mahoney climbed laboriously out of the sack.

Mahoney checked the time. Snorted. It was the middle of the clottin' night. Oh, well. This wouldn't be the first time his boss and interrupted his sleep. And it certainly wouldn't be the last.

He donned his uniform, thought about stalling long enough to grab a Go Cup of caff, but took a look at the long kukri dangling from the little Gurkha's belt and decided against it. He had been told they could lop of a bullock's head with one stroke. Mahoney added this to the fact that the young officer looked as just sleepy and cranky as Mahoney felt and decided this was probably not the best time to test the claim.

The Emperor's study was lit only by a large holoimager at the far side of the room—against a shelf of leather-bound books that only someone like his boss could afford.

As he came closer, he could see that the image was that of the Possnet Sector and what a glorious, but frightening sight it was. Utter desolation amidst a shatter of flaming comets, dying suns and great fiery clouds of rock and ice and dust.

In the center of all this chaos was a large area of relative calm. Objects maintaining sensible orbits. Blips of light showing vessels in transit. Flashing red blips where fighting ships and missiles were kept. And a dozen or more planetoids that had been turned into habitats. This was the Himmenops Colony, where Venatora's women lived.

"That's her fortress," he heard the Emperor say.

Mahoney came closer and found the Emperor sprawled in a long leather couch set in front of the holoimager. He had a shot glass in one hand, which he drained as Mahoney approached.

"Where, sir?" Mahoney asked. "I didn't see where you were pointing.

The Emperor gestured at a dirty gray planetoid at lower edge of the Colony. Mahoney caught it.

"Ah," he said.

"Get yourself a drink, Ian," the Emperor said.

Mahoney nodded. He knew where to go and what to do, which included bringing a bottle back with him. He was guessing stregg.

To his relief the Emperor nodded when he saw the bottle and held out his glass. At this hour, Mahoney's innards weren't ready for Scotch.

Without being asked, he sat on the other end of the couch. Took a honk of his drink. Shudder. God, it was early! Another hit. No. Not yet. Downed the rest. Better now.

Easing back, he refilled his glass and looked over at his boss, hoping he was semi up to his boss' speed.

He said, "I'm supposing she's why you wanted me to have young Sten hang around the Possnet Sector a little longer."

"You supposed right, Ian," the Emperor said. "He's going to have to kill her for me."

"Yessir," Mahoney said. He suppressed a sigh. There had been so much killing of late.

"I know what you're thinking, Ian," the Emperor said. "And I don't like it, either."

"I just wish we had more discretion," Mahoney said. "Some of Gregor's crew were just kids. Didn't know what they were getting themselves into."

"Couldn't agree more," the Emperor said.

"And then there's Gregor—who caused the whole thing," Mahoney added. "And his old man who took it right up to Treason's door and blasted on through it."

"Yep. Looks like they're getting away with everything, doesn't it?" the Emperor said.

"Sometimes it seems like there's no justice to be had," Mahoney said.

"I'm with you, brother," the Emperor said.

He emptied his shot glass and held it out for more. Mahoney complied, not forgetting himself. The fiery Bhor drink had a way settling the world about you. No matter how crazy it was.

"So, instead of putting father and son in front of a firing squad," Mahoney said, "we make them both emissaries to the Tahn. Month or so from now they'll be swilling champagne and noshing finger sandwiches in the finest hotel rooms on Heath."

The Emperor snorted. "You ever been to Heath, Ian?"

Mahoney allowed that he hadn't.

"The Tahn think they are the Spartans reborn," the Emperor said. "Or, closer still, the ancient Samurai. There are no luxuries, much less champagne and finger sandwiches, anywhere near their capital city."

Mahoney made a rude noise. "Wichman's a billionaire," he said. "Probably build one of his resorts on Heath just for himself."

"Wouldn't doubt it," the Emperor said.

Mahoney thought on it for minute or two. Then he said, "I suppose you'll want Sten to kill them too," he said.

"You astound me, Ian," the Emperor said. "Once again, you have supposed correctly."

Mahoney started to chug his stregg, then paused.

"Uh, one other suppose, boss?"

"You have the floor," the Emperor said.

"I'm supposing you want them all gone at the same time. In the same operation. Wichman. Gregor. And Venatora."

"That would be the best way to go," the Emperor said. He paused, then added, "Maybe with fewer casualties this time around. If Sten can manage it, that is. Bloody trails draw suspicious eyes."

"And we don't want the Tahn to catch on, right boss?" Mahoney said.

"That would be my fondest hope," the Emperor said. "But, if he can't, he can't. Don't want to make the job too impossible for him."

"So, killing people is fine, just not too many if he can help it. Are those to be my orders, sir?"

"Exactly so," the Emperor said. "Gregor and his old man shouldn't be too hard a task. Relatively speaking. Sheer clotting greed will no doubt be the end of them."

"I feel bad about the woman," Mahoney said. "I was starting

to grow fond of her."

"So is Sten," the Emperor said. "At least, that's what Rykor said."

"It's a pity she has to die," Ian said. "To cut all that talent and beauty short."

"So it is, Ian," the Emperor said. "So it is."

He knocked back his stregg, took a long breath, then added: "Look at it this way, Ian. The moment she was born, she was old enough to die."

"Sure, boss," Mahoney said. "Sure."

But what he thought was: Except for you, boss. Except for you. And he poured them both another drink.

THE END

Watch for the next Sten adventure,

STEN AND THE PIRATE QUEEN

coming soon!